A VOICE IN THE MIND

The Mind Sleuth Series Book 8

Bruce M. Perrin

Mind Sleuth Publications

First Edition

Cover Art by Courtney M. Perrin

Visit the Author at

brucemperrin.com

ISBN-13: 978-1-955114-10-3 (eBook)

ISBN-13: 978-1-955114-11-0 (Paperback)

For my editor.

*No matter the challenges in her life, she always has time to
remind me that commas aren't the general-purpose,
literary seasoning I think they are.*

Contents

"The night of Friday, the 17th, we had not been long in bed when Robert got up and wrote out a theme that, he said, the angels had sung to him ... Morning came and with it a dreadful change! The angel voices had turned into the voices of demons with horrible music; they told him he was a sinner and they planned to cast him into Hades, in short, his condition increased literally into one of nervous convulsions; he shrieked in pain ..."

CLARA JOSEPHINE SCHUMANN
Renown pianist of the Romantic Era and
wife of Robert Alexander Schumann

TUESDAY, MAY 6

Morning, The Offices of Breakthrough Systems, Denver, CO

Isabella Perez-Hutton badged herself through the front door of the modest office building, no longer feeling the amusement that she had during the first few days on the job. Why, she had wondered back then, did this company need any form of security? They had tried and regularly failed to move their products even when they were giving them away. But after a few days, her levity gave way to concern. If they went out of business due to failing sales, she'd be back on the street looking for another job, and it had taken her months to find this one.

Part of the problem the company faced in establishing its business base was due to the market niche they had chosen—computer-based training for common, albeit somewhat complex software products. Who didn't need a little more instruction on graphics processing applications? Or database software? Or multimedia apps? And if users were into something like simulation, then surely, they'd need some additional training.

But while training on new products such as these was often scarce early in their lifecycle, that vacuum never lasted long. If a product proved useful, the original developer and a host of other independent companies and individuals would soon fill that void. Simply put, their chosen market rapidly became crowded and competitive shortly after each new product release.

The founder and CEO of Breakthrough Systems, however, thought he had found the company's salvation when he decided to create training for writing prompts for artificially intelligent systems. Specifically, he proposed to focus on systems generally known as AI chatbots, such as ChatGPT in its various versions and releases. As a group, they used large language models to understand prompts from a user and to generate descriptions and recommendations based on those requests. What could be a better area for training, he reasoned, when the major tech companies were investing billions and yet didn't fully understand what these chatbots did or how to control them.

Proof of the need for training was readily apparent, at least to the founder and CEO. From the day they were introduced to the public, news stories of these chatbots creating content that sounded factual and yet was pure gibberish appeared with some regularity. These outputs became known as a chatbot's "hallucinations," perhaps because the developers wanted a term that was more positive than "garbage." Surely, the founder of Breakthrough reasoned, a little training on the prompts given to these systems would resolve this problem. And so, he hired Isabella.

It wasn't entirely clear to her, however, whether he had offered her the job because people with a degree in the field were virtually nonexistent—prompt engineering only became a job after ChatGPT was released in late 2022—or because the founder of the company simply didn't understand what she did. She had a master's degree in human factors engineering, which meant she was trained, in part, to design and develop machines that were easier and more intuitive for humans to use. But the irony of her employment at Breakthrough Systems wasn't lost on her. Here, she wouldn't be making machines more intuitive to their human users, but rather, she would be making people's requests more intuitive to the machine.

But whatever the founder's reasoning—or lack thereof—her hiring soon became a masterstroke for the company. As the capabilities of these chatbots became better understood, it was clear that they would, in some cases, replace humans in the workforce. But in many other areas, they would become collaborators with men and women on the job. To do that effectively, people needed to understand chatbots better. That task fell to the tech companies that were developing them ... once they had the answer.

But on the other side of the man-computer partnership, machines needed to understand their human coworkers better. They needed models of their users and their job-related capabilities and limitations so that they didn't recommend anything absurd like asking a one-hundred-fifty-pound worker to reposition a one-ton piece of equipment single-handedly. Some of a human's restrictions were apparent, like physical limitations. But others, such as the ability of a person to hold a series of steps in a maintenance procedure in memory until they could be used depended on a host of variables such as the capacity of working memory, how many independent steps there were in the procedure, and previous experience.

Chatbots also needed to "sell" their recommendations as humans were often leery about taking advice from a computer. How could a chatbot convince a human to take medical advice from it when there were human doctors with years of practice and the intuitions that came from that experience? Or how could one convince a person to take a flight when a computer would be landing the plane rather than a human pilot with in-depth knowledge of the aircraft and reflexes honed by simulation? To make their case, chatbots needed to understand what motivated their human users so that they could list the reasons in terms that humans understood.

And finally, these AI systems needed to engage in less hallucinatory behavior. Since chatbots select the next most likely word or concept based on their training data and what they've produced so far, some degree of hallucination is probably unavoidable. But that's hardly different than a well-educated person misunderstanding a word or concept and so, going off on a tangent. Clearly, however, chatbots could do better than their track record so far.

These three objectives—give advice based on a chatbot's understanding of a problem, get the users to consider and possibly implement that advice, and detect and remove recommendations that are hallucinatory—were the basis for Isabella's job description at Breakthrough Systems. Fortunately, her background in human factors gave her a good foundation, if not specific training for the job.

"Morning, Julia," Isabella said to her second-in-command.

Isabella would never use that title aloud, even though the woman, Julia Morton, was next in line according to the human resources succession plan. To Isabella, it seemed a bit presumptuous for a group of four with no sales so far to have a second-in-command, not to mention a succession plan. But if Eliza was as successful as she hoped, she'd have to adjust her thinking when the staff ballooned to dozens of programmers and support personnel.

Julia was fully qualified for her role as co-lead, both now and in the future. Over the last couple of years, Isabella had left her in charge when she had to be away from work—a need that had never been frequent and was only becoming rarer as the work shifted to the marketing of a nearly complete product. But if Eliza ever became a full-fledged commercial product, Julia was still the right person for the job. In fact, she had been considered for both a programming job and as the team lead. The former job had been offered to her but not the second. Instead, Breakthrough Systems wanted Isabella to head the project with Julia as her backup. Julia had accepted that offer in order to get a break from daily coding.

"Morning, boss. I got that model of human decision-making added to the predictive suite. It looks pretty good, so far."

"That's the one based on the MIT research?"

"It is," Julia replied.

If a chatbot was going to work effectively with a human, it helped to have good models of human behavior, particularly in areas where people were known to make mistakes. Decision-making was one such area. This particular model, developed by MIT and the University of Washington in 2024, conceived of the people's departures from the best solution to be the result of "computational constraints." Simply put, humans couldn't spend hours finding the best possible solution for a single problem. Rather, they took shortcuts, and after observing a person making a few decisions, the model was quite good at predicting the rules of thumb they would apply next. Articles in the popular press often described this model's ability to predict human behavior as "uncanny," so it should be a good addition to the project.

"I suppose at some point," said Isabella, "these chatbots will know where the human will end up even before he or she starts working on a problem."

"Wouldn't surprise me. Members of a team that have worked together for years can often do that. Probably like you and Randy."

Isabella laughed, but not so much from mirth as from tension. She hadn't talked about her deteriorating relationship with her husband to any of her coworkers. She wished she and Randy were closer, but in fact, she had felt more capable of reading his mind when they were first married than she did now, four years later. Back in the early days, if she guessed he was thinking about sex, she'd be right nearly every time. Now, she had no clue, although it was seldom, if ever, about intimacy. A few years ago, he had become reclusive and sullen, even mentioning that he thought he heard voices. Fortunately, that talk had stopped, although it was mostly replaced by silence.

She sighed, only too late realizing that she had done so aloud, so she quickly changed the subject. "I'd be happy if our system got to the right answer eventually."

"No, you wouldn't," retorted Julia with a grin.

"You're right," she admitted with a smile of her own. "Eliza needs to be a lot better than that." She turned and headed for her office.

It wasn't necessarily common for a project lead to name what would eventually become just a component of a software product, but Isabella had named the add-on they were developing "Eliza." It had meaning to her, as it would to those with some background in psychology and artificial intelligence. Eliza was the name of an early natural language processing computer program developed in the mid-1960s at MIT by Joseph Weizenbaum. But it wasn't just homage that Isabella was paying to those who had preceded her in the field. It was also a reminder of a major pitfall she had to avoid. Even though the original Eliza was relatively simple, often just parroting what the user had said in slightly different words, people became emotionally attached to the program. Weizenbaum even told a story of his secretary asking him to leave the room so she could have a heart-to-heart with the computer.

If Isabella wasn't careful, users of her system would declare it conscious and, because Eliza was helpful, a friend. A belief like that, however, was a double-edged sword. Feeling that Eliza was sentient would probably help users accept her advice, but it would also yield views of the software that were invalid and emotions that might prove counterproductive. She didn't want to become known as the developer of everyone's personal confidant in the form of a smart computer, even if there was a demand for such a product.

Rather, Isabella wanted people to see Eliza as a self-adaptive piece of software that responded to their strengths and weaknesses at work. Eliza would know, for example, where her user stood on mastering a given skill and would start her guidance at the appropriate point. Or if a user was getting tired, Eliza's integrated eye-tracking system would detect the change in blink rate and duration and suggest a break. Maybe she could even start a cup of coffee if the coffee machine was controlled via Wi-Fi. And in today's world where everything was networked, the sky was the limit on Eliza's potential to help.

Isabella stepped into her office. "Eliza, what were the results from your last tests on detecting emotional states from images and video?"

"Seventy-nine-point-two percent accuracy in detecting seven emotions in one thousand sixty-two images," said a disembodied female voice coming from a speaker in the corner of her office. "Accuracy from observation of video fell to fifty-six-point-nine percent."

Isabella figured that if she was going to develop capabilities for intelligent machines, who better to help than an AI? So, they had integrated Eliza with several of the commercially available chatbots. Isabella sat down at her desk, nodding in thought.

"Sorry the results weren't better," said Eliza, making Isabella realize that she was probably frowning.

"It's not bad," Isabella replied. "Even humans are only right about ninety percent of the time on pictures and the drop in accuracy from video is to be expected. You have to deal with changes in lighting, occlusion from us turning our heads or someone getting in the way of the camera, and on and on." She paused, chuckling.

"How are you feeling at this moment?"

"Yes, Eliza, that was amusement because I'm sitting here in my office explaining why the drop in accuracy is expected when those are research results that you already know."

The machine's question—how are you feeling—was all too common to Isabella, as well as everyone on her team. When she had decided that she needed something closer to real-life emotion identification than what she could get from the chatbot analyzing still pictures and video clips, she had asked her coworkers and her husband if they minded being recorded and asked about their emotional state from time to time.

Initially, they had all agreed, but it soon became clear that she had set the sampling rate too high. They all complained that it was like being followed around by a toddler, who, instead of saying "Watch me, watch me" said, "How are you feeling, how are you feeling?" It got on people's nerves. So, she reduced the sampling, which helped. Even so, one of her team, Calvin Whitmer, her programmer, had dropped out permanently. And her husband? He only seemed to describe his emotion as "thoughtful" and little else. Those losses were unfortunate and made more so because there were generally large differences in emotion recognition between the genders. But she'd make do with just the data from Julia, Molly Reynolds, and herself until she could expand the study.

Molly Reynolds, Isabella thought with a shake of her head. Now, there was a trooper. Julia, with her software background, led integration and test. Calvin supplied the computer code Eliza required. And Molly ... well, she did everything else. She managed the documentation, drafted reports, and reviewed the software builds for quality. She even kept their small galley stocked with coffee, even though no one had asked her to do that. Where would they be ...

"It's almost time to meet with your group," said Eliza, breaking into Isabella's thoughts.

Using Eliza as an alarm clock was an extreme underutilization of an intelligent system, but it was a function Isabella valued. When she was first married, Randy had teased her that she'd forget her head if it wasn't tied on. Yes, it was an extremely tired quip, but she missed it along with everything else that he no longer joked about. But the old adage was also accurate. She did tend to get lost in her own mental world, only surfacing when someone, like Eliza, called upon her.

"Thanks," she said to the machine, opening the notebook on her desktop to refresh her memory of the group's action items. She'd need to ask Julia to expand upon her comments about the human behavior prediction model. And then, they'd all have to listen as Calvin explained how incredibly complex its integration had been. If he ever said that a task had been easy-peasy, she thought the rest of the group might faint. And finally, she'd have Molly describe ... well, whatever she had been doing recently since it seemed like she was constantly manning two or three jobs and Isabella wasn't certain what her current priorities were.

Julia and Calvin entered her office. "So, when are we going to get digs big enough to have a real meeting room rather than just your office?" Calvin asked.

"As people who are familiar with the field know ..." Isabella kicked herself mentally for the start of her statement, repeating a phrase that she had found herself using often even though it wasn't fair to Calvin. In many ways, the requirement for him to stretch his skills was no different than her need to flip the script from making machines intuitive to people to making users intuitive to machines. Calvin's background was typical software engineering and included math, a sampling of programming languages, operating systems, and so on. Where he might have specialized in AI, he'd studied networking, a generally valuable area of specialization even if it wasn't crucial for their project. But he was getting the job done, a fact that she needed to recognize rather than implying he wasn't the right fit.

Since Isabella couldn't take back the words she had already uttered, she added, "And I'm sure you recognize, Calvin, that the tools and training to fill the prompt engineering void are appearing all the time. To stand out in what will soon be a crowd, we need hard data. Fortunately, we are only months away from having that proof."

"Months? By then ..."

Calvin stopped, staring at Molly who was now standing in the doorway. When Isabella followed his gaze, she was certain he'd never get back to his thoughts. Molly was crying softly, her entire body pulsing to sobs she couldn't control.

"Molly, how are you feeling at this moment?"

"Shut up, Eliza," Isabella snapped. "Molly, what's wrong?"

"You," said Molly. "You're wrong."

Molly's words were a mix of sounds that Isabella recognized and an odd gurgling noise that made them nearly unintelligible. Isabella leaned forward straining to understand what her coworker was saying. "I don't ... I don't know what you mean."

"Yes, you wouldn't." Molly swayed dangerously close to collapse but reached a hand out to the doorframe just in time.

"I've been working my butt off, trying to make a difference. Not for this group. Not for frickin' Eliza or these stupid chatbots. But for you." Molly squeezed her eyes closed, a tear running down a cheek and onto lips that had turned dark blue. A pained grimace distorted her features.

"And we all appreciate your efforts," said Isabella, hastening to add, "especially me."

"I don't want ..." Molly slumped back against the doorframe, her gaze starting to wander aimlessly around the room.

"Molly, did you take something?" Isabella demanded. She stood from her desk and stepped closer, hoping the woman would tell them what they were up against.

When Molly's eyes returned to her boss, they registered surprise even though she had looked away for only an instant. She paused to take a breath but failed as she gagged with the effort. "I don't want your damn appreciation. I wanted your love."

"But I'm ..." started Isabella.

"You're what? Married? Anyone who knows you knows your marriage is a sham. And I, I could have made you ..." Molly coughed. The exertion, however, was too much and she slid down the doorframe to the floor and laid there without moving.

Isabella stepped forward and slapped Molly's cheek, hoping the pain would bring her back to consciousness. It didn't. If Molly was breathing, Isabella couldn't detect it even though she was now crouched nearby, her ear just inches from the woman's mouth. She tried to check for a pulse, but since she had no training, she wasn't sure if Molly had none or if she couldn't find it.

"Calvin, call 9-1-1." But when she looked at the programmer, he was just standing there with his mouth half open as if he didn't understand what was happening.

"Julia, you call," shouted Isabella.

Somewhere in her long ago past, Isabella had learned CPR. Now, she wished she'd had more practice. But failing to find any breath, she tilted Molly's head back, pinched off her nose, and breathed into her mouth twice. Then, she compressed Molly's chest thirty times before repeating the cycle of breaths and compression.

In a few minutes, building security showed up and took over for her. All Isabella could do was stand back and let them work while tears ran down her cheeks.

Morning, The Huttons' Apartment, Denver, CO

Isabella had left for work nearly two hours earlier, but Randy Hutton, as he was prone to do these days, was finding it difficult to pull himself out of bed. After all, it wasn't like his wife needed his help to get ready. In fact, staying out of her way was probably the best thing he could do for her and he was becoming an expert at that.

When she was working—which was nearly all the time—he didn't step into her "home office," a small alcove that held a desk, computer, and filing cabinet. He didn't bore her with idle chitchat over dinner, often eating his meal after she had gone to bed. But most of all, he didn't disturb her sleep with unrequited sexual advances; he was just too tired to try, not that it would lead to anything anyway. That ship had sailed long ago.

Now, all he sought from her was to be left alone, which she did, for the most part, as long as he kept the house in immaculate order. The guest bedroom, however, was his, and immaculate was the last word anyone would use to describe it. It was a pigsty filled with half-eaten meals, dirty dishes, and porn, all with the air that only filthy laundry could provide. So, he kept the door locked to make sure that nothing disturbed the equilibrium between grimy and gleaming.

Randy heaved himself out of the bed, stepped to a window, and pulled back a corner of the blackout shades. Brilliant sunlight stabbed his eyes and he winced in pain. Perhaps he had once, too, shared his wife's passion for light, but now all it did was reveal the ugliness of his life. He pushed the blinds back into place. "Another beautiful day in this damn hellhole," he muttered to himself.

He checked his attire. It was the same pair of boxers he had worn for the last … well, he couldn't recall how many days it had been, but it was time to change. He was starting to smell, and the only thing worse than not sleeping was one of his wife's lectures. "You really should take better care of yourself," she would say mildly when the odor reached her nose, keeping the dark, vicious thoughts that were driving those words hidden. But he knew what she thought of him.

He kicked off his shorts into an overflowing trash can and retrieved a clean pair from a new pack. He'd found that it was much easier to buy new skivvies in bulk than to wash the dirty ones, as laundry was something his wife demanded of him to earn his keep. True, the quality of this underwear was abysmal, but they lasted the week or two necessary. And by ordering cheaper cuts of meat in their delivered groceries—something he passed off to Isabella as the overall deterioration of the country after the pandemic—she was never the wiser.

He trudged into their living room, pulling the drapes closed. He slowly surveyed his modest surroundings, modest because they had to live on his wife's income alone. That was a fact he could never forget because …

Finally decided to get out of bed, you lousy piece of …

"Good morning to you, too, Schumann," Randy snarled to the voice that came from deep inside his head. "I need a break."

Oh, poor baby. Of course, you need a break from lying in bed half the day and sitting on your butt the rest. Why didn't you say so?

When the voice had first started, Randy wasn't sure he had heard anything, much less, a voice. But over a week or two, it became more distinct. He thought it was just part of what his wife was doing to test the software she was creating at work. After all, she had the whole place wired with microphones, cameras, and speakers. "All the better to get some data that is closer to the real world," she had said. But when he asked her about the sounds that had become a voice, she had claimed to know nothing.

At first, Randy wasn't sure he believed her. After all, she had that damn assistant—what was her name? Ella? Elsie? Eliza. That was it. It seemed to know everything he did, following him around, asking how he felt all the time. But the voice he heard was male. And if Isabella knew anything about it, she was playing the naivety card masterfully. She even offered to record the sounds in the house when she was at work. And when they listened to them together, all they heard was him shuffling around in his bare feet, snoring when he took a nap, and talking to himself the rest of the time.

Don't tell that bitch of a wife of yours that you hear voices, Schumann had warned him shortly after that. *She'll have you locked up and throw away the key.* And so, he kept his mouth shut. Confinement with people like himself was a thought he couldn't stand. They'd all be talking to voices only they could hear. And so, Schumann became Randy's secret.

"Where did you get the name Schumann?" asked Randy, thinking that directing the conversation toward the voice might spare him some of its venom. "I don't know anyone by that name."

With your complete lack of formal education in the fine arts, it's not surprising you don't recognize the name, replied Schumann. *Robert*

Alexander Schumann was one of the most famous Romantic composers of the nineteenth century. Often, his voices would bring him complete compositions of exquisite melodies. But sometimes, he'd try to improve on perfection and those same entities would have to punish him with visions of Hades and nights filled with pain.

But then, I just use Schumann's name. I'm not him. Actually, I'm you, the permanent leech on your wife's good nature and generosity. So, to answer your question, all I need to do is hold up a mirror so you can see the worthless drag on humanity that you are.

Randy knew that Schumann's words were true. He was a complete and utter failure. At first, his life had been filled with promise. He'd risen quickly to first-level management in a customer service department for a national shipping company. Unfortunately, almost exactly one month after he and Isabella were married, he lost that job. "A victim of technology," his supervisor had said during his exit interview.

At the time, the technology that displaced him had been nothing more than a somewhat elaborate voicemail system. Supposedly, it was going to handle the routine cases—my package is lost; it was supposed to be here this morning. That would leave him time to tackle the complex issues. But in reality, there weren't many tough problems, and the new system could handle nearly all of the work. So, with that early success, the company invested even more in automation. Soon, a department of twenty became a staff of one, and there was no need for a first-level manager.

Randy knew that the minor cut in jobs at the shipping company would be nothing compared to the chopping block that artificial intelligence would be for the workforce. And paradoxically, his wife was one of those with her hand on the butcher's cleaver. He didn't need Schumann to point out the irony of that fact.

"But you did say there was something in my future."

So I did.

"Don't you think it's about time you told me what it is?" asked Randy. "Or is dishing out vitriol all you can do?"

Oh, I can do much more. So much more.

"Then, do it!"

At this point, Randy was nearly shouting, and he took a furtive glance at the common wall between their apartment and Mrs. Masterson's place. She was an ancient busybody who probably had 9-1-1 on speed dial because she couldn't remember the number. She had used that number once for him when all he had done was answer the door in his boxers. He knew it was her at the door, had seen her through the peephole. He'd even considered pulling his privates out of his shorts before he opened it to see if she'd die from shock ... but he hadn't. Even so, that hadn't kept her from calling the police.

"Not any different than what I'd wear to the beach," he muttered to himself, although that fact hadn't kept his wife from berating him for days about the incident.

"We have to live with these people whether we like them or not," she'd replied.

Not necessarily, he had thought at the time but hadn't said.

After a moment, Randy realized that Schumann hadn't answered him. That was strange. He was usually so prompt in sharing his loathing. "Schumann?"

Still, nothing. Usually, Randy could sense when Schumann had left, but this time, he wasn't sure. Could it be that the voice that had haunted him day and night, that had stripped the façade of hope and promise from his life had finally had enough? And if so, what had been the final straw? What was the truth that had laid bare his futility and uselessness once and for all? Randy tried to recall Schumann's final words, but already they were fading into the quagmire of past recriminations.

Suddenly, Randy's hand went to his throat as he realized he couldn't breathe. He reached out for the arm of their living room sofa, nearly missing it as the room started to spin. He fell onto it, his eyes searching the corners of the darkened room for the evil he knew lived there. Would Schumann become physical? Did he need actual hands to smother the last fading embers of his life? He started to sweat, bile rising in his throat to close the last vestiges of an airway. Searing pain erupted from his chest as he tore at his own skin to release the demon within.

Easy, Randy, came Schumann's voice. *I do have plans for you.*

The pain lifted from Randy's body with those six words. Air once again flowed to his lungs. His racing heart slowed.

So you won't doubt my word when I reveal your destiny, I'll give you tonight, said Schumann. *When you lie down in bed, you'll sleep, long and peaceful. You'll wake up fully rested, a gift from me.*

"OK," Randy replied slowly. Although Schumann never spoke to him when he was in bed, he always had that perfect parting remark to rob Randy of rest. "What is it that I have to do to get a night of peace?"

Nothing for yourself, but rather, a mission for all mankind.

"For all mankind?" said Randy. "Could you be any more cryptic?"

I'll be crystal clear when the time comes. But for now, here's something that you can get your literal head around. Any moment now, you'll get a call from Breakthrough Systems. Isabella is fine, but there's been a death in her team. Molly Reynolds, if you know the name.

"Not really," Randy replied with a shrug. Perhaps he should have been more interested in his wife's coworkers, but they talked about a lot of crap that made no sense to him.

Pity, said Schumann. *Attractive girl. Young. Well endowed. You could have fantasized about her when you relieved your sexual tensions.*

"Jeez, Schumann. Don't I get any privacy?"

Isabella is upset, Schumann said, ignoring Randy's complaint. *They're taking her to the hospital, and if they are even halfway competent, they'll keep her overnight for observation. Even if you don't know Molly, your wife will feel like she's lost her right arm. Molly was one of the true believers.*

"True believers?" said Randy. "What are you talking about?"

So, in addition to a night of peaceful sleep, should you decide to use it, said Schumann, again ignoring Randy's question, *I also give you an empty apartment. Rather than dreaming, you could decide to call some hookers and take advantage of the space. Or get Marianne Olsen from the next building to come over, assuming you're not too much of a coward. I've seen the way you ogle her; you could have a drunken orgy. Anyway, this is my gift, and you can use it as you desire.*

But make no mistake, said Schumann. *As easily as I can grant you this night of freedom, I can take it away. I can plunge you deeper into your own personal hell than you could ever imagine and leave you there for eternity. So, until tomorrow ...*

Schumann was gone. Randy could feel it this time. His thoughts were now his own. Even so, he looked around the room, checking every nook and cranny. He'd never seen Schumann before, but then, that didn't mean he was invisible, did it?

Randy pressed his head between the palms of his hands. What the hell was he supposed to do? He'd been offered a night of restful slumber, but his wife was going to the hospital. Or was Schumann mistaken about that? He'd never been wrong before, but then, perhaps the phantom in his head only had insight into his failings, not the goings on in a building eight miles away.

If Isabella's work called and she was being taken to the hospital—he still wasn't sure he believed Schumann's story—shouldn't he spend the night there by her side? He didn't think he could. What if he talked in his sleep? Or worse, what if Schumann came to torment him further? He couldn't just sit there and take it with nurses and doctors coming and going at all hours of the night. No, he'd make an appearance and then, an excuse. The last thing he needed was a bunch of quacks who'd want to x-ray his head to make sure something alien wasn't living there.

Randy jumped when his phone rang. No name appeared on the display, but then, he'd never bothered adding Breakthrough Systems to his contacts. Why should he? They wouldn't call him. With a shaky hand, he accepted the call.

"Hello," he said slowly.

"Mr. Hutton?"

"Yes."

"This is Diane Chang at Breakthrough Systems. Isabella is fine, but as a precaution, we've called an ambulance for her. You see …"

Randy heard nothing more because he already knew what she was going to say.

WEDNESDAY, MAY 7

Morning, The Huttons' Apartment

Randy gritted his teeth, knowing that he was fighting a losing battle against his bladder.

For reasons he didn't understand but treasured, Schumann never assailed him in the guest bedroom; unfortunately, however, it didn't have an ensuite bathroom and he needed to go in the worst way. It was true that he had made several trips throughout the night, one lasting a half hour or more as he passed out with his head hanging over the toilet. Perhaps he'd gotten away with those excursions because no one, even Schumann, would have been able to penetrate the alcoholic fog that enveloped his mind. But that protective mist had evaporated with the rising sun.

He slipped out of bed, tiptoeing toward the bathroom as if stealth would make a difference.

You're even more pathetic than I ever imagined, said Schumann.

"Can't you get out of my head for a moment?"

Do you mean like this?

This time, the voice had come from behind, so Randy spun around, expecting to finally meet his nemesis face-to-face. The sudden movement, however, was too much. The room tilted wildly as he fell to the floor, his bladder emptying in the wake of the pain from a twisted knee. "Damn you, Schumann."

Said the man who just peed his pants. Once again, the voice came from inside his head. *I give you a night of blissful sleep. I offer you the opportunity to use more than your hand to satisfy your carnal cravings, and what do you do but pass out in a drunken stupor. How pathetic can you be?*

"The night was mine to use as I wanted," said Randy, although he knew he hadn't chosen the bottle; it had picked him. He started out thinking that after one swallow, he'd have the nerve to find some female companionship. Then, one more because the kind of woman he needed was streetwise; she'd recognize him for what he was without the bravado provided by the booze. But somehow, his need for "just one more" had never ended. "Yeah, I didn't make very good use of your gift, did I?" Randy admitted.

Finally, the bit of self-awareness I've been waiting for. It's time for the first step toward realizing a modicum of your potential.

"What?" Randy had been sure that last night's performance would delay or maybe even prevent his rescue from the nightmare that his life had become. "You're going to help me?"

I'm going to show you the way, said Schumann. But you're going to have to help yourself.

"I'll do anything."

We'll see, said the voice. You are about to receive a call from your wife. A shrink has recommended that she and another coworker named Julia, take a couple of days away from their lives. After some discussion with the company's president, Isabella agreed.

Schumann paused. *It's interesting, don't you think, that she didn't call you for your input?*

Randy didn't find it all that strange. "Calling can be such a ...

Whatever, said Schumann, apparently not interested in his explanation. *Since your only car is at Breakthrough Systems, the president will be picking her and Julia up at the hospital and dropping them off at work. Then, Isabella will drive directly to where she will be spending a couple of nights.*

"Where's that?" asked Randy.

A shelter for victims of violence called Jen's Place, but that's irrelevant to you. You have other plans for the evening.

"I do?"

Indeed, you do, replied Schumann. *While she's decompressing in her new surroundings, you'll be wrecking her lab.*

"What? Why would I do that?"

You know why, replied Schumann.

At first, Randy thought the infallible Schumann was wrong. Why would he destroy months of his wife's labor? But slowly, thoughts buried deep in his subconscious began to clamor for recognition. Scenes from dinner parties with new acquaintances, nearly forgotten over the last two years, came rushing back.

"Randy, what do you do?" one of them would ask.

"My husband is currently between jobs. He's just waiting for the right opportunity," Isabella would answer before he could open his mouth.

He had no idea why she said that and feared that one day, one of them would ask, "And what does this opportunity look like?" He had no clue since helping losers find their missing package didn't develop a lot of transferable skills. Hell, he now knew that it was so simple even a machine could do it.

So, he and Isabella had stopped going out with the people she met, and the first of her many disenchantments with him came to be.

Their socializing with friends lasted a bit longer, but eventually, even the best of them had enough. Perhaps it was because he started answering their queries with, "Currently, I'm adjusting my work-life balance, checking the all-life-no-work option first." He figured what they heard was, "None of your damn business," because that's what he meant. And so, Isabella continued to meet with several of them for lunch where he was certain his name never came up.

It wasn't that he gave up on his life immediately after losing his customer service job. He had tried a few others, but soon after starting each, he realized that the costs and inconveniences of his working nearly or totally offset his meager pay. Meanwhile, Isabella was becoming the darling of Breakthrough Systems. Her salary hadn't caught up with the kudos she was receiving, but soon he figured it would look like the trend line on a viral social media post.

He had tried gig work from home. He'd even proudly announced his first foray into the arena to Isabella. But when it failed, as all of the freelancing work he tried invariably did, he told her at dinner that at least he had only wasted a little of his time.

"I'm sorry it didn't work out," Isabella had said, but in Randy's mind he heard the cliché, "Time is money," with the addition, "but apparently, your time is worthless."

And then, he'd watch as she got up from the table to invest some of her own personal time in her home office to make more of the money that he couldn't. But then, that wasn't quite right, was it? His failed ventures into the commercial world had a cost even if it was just measured in chores around the house that didn't get done because of them.

"I had to stop working to stop the bleeding," Randy muttered to himself.

What was that? asked Schumann. Randy just waved him off in reply.

It wasn't like Isabella didn't know that his work came with a price tag rather than a paycheck. A few weeks after his final debacle—an attempt to sell custom mirrors online for which he had more breakage than product—she suggested that he run the household. He recalled the talk like it was yesterday.

"You want me to be a ... househusband?" he had asked.

"Something will come along eventually. But in the meantime, running our home will take some of the pressure off. It'll give you a chance to relax."

He knew what she meant, but even if he hadn't, Schumann gave him the precise translation a few days later. *You're good for nothing, so why not do nothing?*

Then later, Isabella had said, "You'll probably have time to take a few classes, maybe at the community college."

Once again, Schumann translated the next day: *You're not the brightest bulb, but maybe a class or two can hide a few of the most glaring rough spots.*

"And besides," she had said, "I make enough money for us to get by." She paused. "That is, as long as we sell your car. I don't think we can afford two. When we're down to one car, you can order the groceries online for delivery. And get anything else you need the same way. To get gas for the lawn mower, it's only a couple of blocks to walk to a gas station. And you can pay the bills online, too."

Schumann didn't need to translate that one for him, but he did anyway. *You don't even need to show your face outside the apartment.*

That way, your charming wife could even tell her friends that you're dead if she wants to. And she probably will.

Reluctantly, Randy had agreed, thinking it was just a temporary solution. But nearly two years later, the only thing that had changed in his job description was that he had found a teenager up the street to clear the snow from behind their assigned carport. After all, he couldn't afford for her to be late to work or to lose a finger to frostbite. That would put even more strain on her paltry paycheck.

Randy pulled his mind back to the present, spotting a problem in Schumann's proposal to wreck his wife's lab as he refocused. "They just had a death at Breakthrough. The place will be crawling with cops."

It was a suicide, not a murder, Schumann replied without trying to hide the exasperation in his tone. *She OD'd on a prescription for pain pills from her doctor, so while the cops will probably have some questions for him, no one is looking at anyone at Breakthrough Systems.*

"You're sure about that?" Randy waited several moments, but it became clear that Schumann wasn't going to bother justifying his assertion.

"OK," Randy said eventually. "But that still leaves the question of security. I won't get past the front door without a badge and Isabella is never without hers. And then there's the cameras all over the place."

The cameras you're worried about are in the lab, but they won't be on. Work on Eliza has been paused until your wife comes back into the office. And since the security at Breakthrough is relatively new, the only other cameras are on the loading dock. Stay clear of them. As for badging in at the front door, I'll take care of that. Just run your driver's license through the reader.

"Are you nuts? I might as well take a selfie of me wrecking the lab."

Their security's not going to record anything off your driver's license. I just need to know it's you before I open the door.

If the voice suddenly became physical and occupied a space in Randy's reality, he would have turned away. He was starting to feel angry. He was being bullied into a situation where he had no control. And even if the voice knew and could do everything it said, he was still the only one taking a risk, the only one who could go to jail. Why did he even think he could trust Schumann's word?

"You sure seem to know a lot about where my wife works," Randy said as a preamble to telling Schumann he wasn't going to destroy the lab, but he got no further.

You would, too, if she ever gave you a chance.

"What do you mean?" asked Randy. "She's never done anything to keep me down."

You think not, do you? She and the other true believers have a name for you and your kind—the expendables. You never had a chance even before your mom kicked you out of the house. You never had a chance even before you killed those dogs. You never had a chance even before you were ousted by a machine.

"Isabella had nothing to do with me losing my job," objected Randy. "I got replaced by a frickin' answering machine."

And you think the carnage to come due to intelligent computer systems taking over people's jobs will be less? You are just the tip of that iceberg.

"And why is that my problem?"

It's not your problem, replied Schumann. It's your opportunity. All you need to do is slow her down. Soon, those who are rational in government will see through the greed of corporations, and humankind will be spared the merciless onslaught of automation.

"Don't you think you're being a little melodramatic?" asked Randy.

You know you've become part of the dregs of humanity because of some really low-level automation, a frickin' answering machine as you put it, said Schumann in return. *Now, extrapolate that to machines that hold all of the accumulated knowledge of the world and tell me if I'm being too melodramatic.*

Randy had to admit, Schumann had a point. The issues, however, were complex. Or was he just being the coward that Schumann and Isabella believed him to be? He wasn't sure.

Look, said Schumann. *I'm not going to debate it with you. Do what you should by slowing her down a few months or don't. It makes no difference to me. But if you decide to be a man, then take a taxi to a spot a few blocks from Breakthrough, get out there, and walk the rest of the way. Badge yourself in with your license and go to her lab. It's on the fourth floor, room 414. Destroy everything you find there, and you should have given the government a couple of months to come to their senses. Good luck.*

Again, Randy knew Schumann was gone, that feeling of a void in his mind returning. Even without further thought, he knew he really had no choice. If he did nothing, his waking nightmare would only get worse. So, he was going out tonight to do what had to be done.

Late Morning, Jen's Place, Lone Tree, CO

Nicole Veles skimmed the admissions form for the woman sitting across the desk from her.

"So, Nicole, you run Jen's Place?" asked the woman.

"That's correct … Mrs. Perez-Hutton," Nicole replied, using the pause to find the woman's name on the document before looking up. "Only for a few months now, but it's home … for me and the women and children who stay here." She returned her gaze to the pages in front of her.

"Please, call me Isabella. I can't have you calling me Mrs. Hutton if I'm supposed to be calling you Nicole."

"I'd be pleased to, Isabella," Nicole replied as she looked up again. She wondered if there was any significance to the fact that the woman hadn't used her hyphenated name with the request when apparently, she did use it on official documents. But not seeing any immediate relevance, she returned to the paperwork in front of her.

"And these are your private quarters?" asked Isabella.

Once again, Nicole looked up, wondering if the surroundings were, for some reason, making Isabella uneasy. Or was it something else? It seemed like it had to be something more than just idle curiosity since she kept calling her away from the admissions form. "Correct. It seemed like it would be a waste to take a room for an office when I'd rarely use it, especially when this room is so big. So, I moved a desk in here. And my door is always open, for business or just to talk."

Nicole didn't immediately return her gaze to the form because Isabella's eyes had narrowed in thought. She was leading up to something although Nicole still had no idea what it might be.

"I'm not really a victim of domestic abuse," said Isabella after a moment. "But then, I suppose you know that already." She waved a hand at the paperwork.

So, that was it, thought Nicole. Isabella wasn't sure she belonged here. Nicole smiled as she pushed the document over to where Isabella could read it. "As you can see, all I really have is basic contact and descriptive information for you—name, age, gender, address—plus anything specific I need to know about your stay, such as dietary restrictions. That section, which is toward the bottom, is blank. Otherwise, all I really know is that my guests have been victims of some type of violence, which is often domestic but not always."

"So … So, that comes out during our counseling sessions?" asked Isabella.

"It would, except I'm not a clinician. You and I won't be meeting." Nicole turned the form to face her for a moment, then back to Isabella. "It looks like your referral came from Dr. Rose Martens. She's good. She can continue with you here if you want. Or we have a counselor who runs two group sessions a week funded by the state. Those sessions are completely discretionary and deal with coping with stress in general, so they are appropriate for virtually all of our guests. You'll find more information on those sessions in your room."

"I'll pass," Isabella replied, then smiled. "I suppose it's a good thing you told me you aren't a counselor as quickly as I turned down that offer."

"I had a brush with violence a couple of years ago and met with a counselor for a while afterward," said Nicole. "But with the friends I've made after moving here, I'm like you—I don't feel the need anymore." Nicole saw the flicker of a grimace pass across Isabella's features when she used the phrase, "brush with violence." She thought the woman might ask what had happened but hoped not. Something in common with her guests would probably help build rapport, but the details would just create emotional baggage that none of them needed. And so, Nicole had never shared her story with any of her guests. For that matter, she hadn't shared it with anyone in the area, preferring anonymity to the questions her past would raise.

"Yeah, my support network's pretty good, too," Isabella said, apparently deciding that her question about Nicole's past, if she had one, was too personal. "My family's mostly back in Des Moines, but my mom and I talk all the time. And Julia, a coworker, is a rock. Course, I thought the same about Calvin, the other member of my team, but he split after the incident at work and no one has seen him since. Then, there's my mother-in-law. I know that runs counter to many wives' experiences, but we're pretty close. And, of course, my husband." She paused a beat. "But I suppose I'm a bit of a mystery to most of our neighbors. My work keeps me pretty busy."

"Same here," said Nicole. "I handle quite a bit of the maintenance of the building and grounds and the daily operations of the shelter. But the paperwork? That's the killer. And in my off-hours, I do part-time work for a biomedical engineering company called HealthVie."

"Really?" said Isabella, her eyes narrowing. "I know that company. What do you do for them?"

"Design mostly, but a bit of testing, too."

"No way! You're a biomedical engineer! That is ... well, quite an achievement."

Nicole had heard surprise in the voices of others she had told, but that came mostly from men. Many of the women just stared at her blankly before changing the subject. The fact that Isabella found her part-time work interesting was not a reaction she expected. "I was full-time before and loved the field. It's a chance to help people. But then, things changed and this opportunity came along. Now, I work for HealthVie to help people's bodies cope with life and here to help their minds do the same ... although the mental healthcare professionals get most of the credit for the latter."

"Unbelievable. I work in a related field." Isabella paused. "Well, that's being somewhat presumptuous I suppose, because it's not really anything as rigorous as biomedical engineering." She released a single laugh. "In fact, I've had people tell me I should have changed my degree to a real engineering discipline, quote-unquote, before I graduated."

Isabella's disclaimers had gone on long enough that Nicole was starting to wonder if the woman was going to name her profession or not when she said, "I'm a human-factors engineer, modeling how people learn and think so humans and intelligent systems can be more effective teammates." Isabella laughed. "Sorry, I just tossed in one of the lines from my tiny group's sales brochure, but that's the gist of what we do."

"So, you're developing artificial intelligence systems?" Nicole asked slowly.

"No, not the AIs themselves. That's falling to the multi-billion-dollar tech companies who can foot the immense bills for electricity. I head a team that is developing a front-end to them, a component that understands how the user likes to work and that can explain why its recommendations are the best way to go."

"OK. That makes sense." But there was something in Isabella's earlier statement that didn't. "In biomedical engineering, I may work in microns, but then, I get data in microns, not in thoughts or intentions or emotions. Just who in the world told you that human factors wasn't a real engineering discipline anyway because, as a good friend of mine often says, what could be more challenging than studying the human mind?"

"That would be my husband, actually," said Isabella, "but the comment was before we were married."

"Well, I assume you've enlightened him over the years." Nicole paused, pondering the question she wanted to ask. She didn't usually engage her guests in conversations about their lives outside of Jen's Place. There were just too many potential landmines in those talks. But somehow, Isabella seemed different. "Say, are you free to describe some of your work if I promise I won't take it to HealthVie and run with it?"

Isabella laughed. "No, please take this back to their lab. I'd love to have more solutions and fewer questions."

Her expression turned more serious. "Well, we just finished integrating software that simulates human biases in decision-making. Adding that was an easy call. For example, you'd want an intelligent system to know when their human teammate was about to overestimate the likelihood of something because it's easy for them to recall examples of it—like thinking driving is safer than flying because of the dramatic media coverage of plane crashes. That's a judgment bias called availability."

"I think I could have recalled the term availability ... although I get it confused with representativeness sometimes," said Nicole. "Neither is anything that comes up in biomedical engineering, but that friend I mentioned before? He talks about those biases ... and others."

"Really? Other than people who work in decision-support, like me, I don't hear people talking much about human judgment biases. What's he do for a living?"

"He's a cognitive psychologist. He mostly does research on training technology for a company named Ruger-Phillips."

"Yeah, I can see why judgment bias is something he would be interested in." Isabella rubbed her chin for a moment. "And with his background in applied research, he could probably help us. We keep using these psychological models that are good at describing group behavior—on average, people overestimate the risk of flying—but they don't necessarily describe any one person that well. Some people are more prone to this error, others less so. So, to adjust the models, my programmer tries to collect data on how often Eliza's advice influences the actions of our team. Four of us, including my husband, are being monitored and advised by Eliza. The trouble is ..."

Isabella stopped midsentence and chuckled. "Damn, I'm incorrigible. Here I am in this peaceful setting where I'm supposed to be relaxing, and instead, I'm working. And worse, I'm speculating about how your friend, who I have never even met, might be able to help. I'm sorry."

"No need to be. His company has an office in Denver, but he's based in St. Louis. Even so, if you want to brainstorm ideas on a phone call, I can do the introductions."

"You're very generous with his time," Isabella replied.

"Not really. He enjoys all the modeling and statistical stuff. But there's a downside in involving him."

"Oh, yeah? What's that?"

"If you get him started, it might be tough to get him to stop."

Isabella laughed. "You know, I should have thought about your background before I gave my example of what we are doing with Eliza. We have a lot of physiological checks built into the system, too." She paused a beat. "For example, if a sound that is important to a task is at the lower end of humans' auditory sensitivity, an intelligent system can make sure the person heard it. Or it could replay the sound for them at a higher volume. And since we can input individual sensitivity profiles into the system, it works for the person who's a bit hard of hearing, too."

"Or someone who's lost some sensitivity in one ear?" asked Nicole.

"Actually, we hadn't considered that yet," said Isabella slowly, "but there's no reason why we couldn't. We already have multiple microphones in our test suites, so the machine would know the direction the sound is coming from by comparing when it reaches each of the microphones. If it was coming into the person's weaker ear, then the system could ask to make sure it was heard." Isabella paused, nodding a couple of times. "I'm pretty sure that enhancement will end up on our schedule when I get back in the office. Would a footnote in the technical specifications be enough recognition for you?"

"I don't think that's even worth a footnote," Nicole said with a chuckle. She spun the form around once again to check something. "It looks like you're only here for two days and I have something I need to do later today. But would you be interested in getting together again, maybe this evening at dinner, to talk some more?"

"You're enjoying this nerd-speak?" Isabella asked.

"Absolutely," replied Nicole. "Sometimes I go into the HealthVie lab just to talk about some of the latest biomedical research. I get so wrapped up in the discussion that they have to kick me out at closing time."

Isabella laughed. "I don't believe that for a minute, but yes, dinner tonight would be great."

Evening, Jen's Place

"I can't believe I ate all of that stew, but it was wonderful," said Isabella as she leaned back in her chair and placed her hands on the table so they flanked the bowl that was empty save one small crust of bread. "If your cook ever wants a change of scenery for a night, you can send her over to my place."

"I'll let her know you liked it," replied Nicole. "But, at least in my opinion, you're in for a real treat tomorrow night. She's making meatloaf. And, yeah, I know. Meatloaf is the punchline of a hundred jokes about awful food, but hers is really good. Not like mine, which is usually a complete disaster."

"I'm sure you're exaggerating," said Isabella.

"Let's just say that if feeding the guests was my responsibility, I could bill Jen's Place as a weightwatcher's shelter."

"Yeah, I'm not that good of a cook either," Isabella admitted after a moment. "I just never really had the time to learn and now, Randy—that's my husband—he does most of the cooking. He's not very good, either, so we end up with a lot of carry-out or frozen entrees from the grocery store."

"I've never asked her before, but I can see if Josey would share some of her recipes."

"Recipes we have. Time and the inclination to work with them, not so much." Isabella reached out for the remaining crust of bread and picked it up.

"So, your husband keeps pretty busy, too?"

Nicole knew immediately she had accidentally stumbled into a sensitive area as Isabella dropped the uneaten bread back into the bowl. Then, she let her hands drop to her lap as her eyes followed them to their new resting place.

"When you checked in this morning, I mentioned that I wasn't a counselor," said Nicole. "And I just proved it. I shouldn't be poking around in people's personal lives."

Isabella had looked up when Nicole first spoke and now, she held her gaze for a moment. "And I mentioned that I wasn't the victim of domestic abuse … and I'm not," she added quickly. "But things haven't always gone like Randy and I planned."

"Life can have its challenges," Nicole said, using the first platitude that came to mind. "But it sounds like you've met and mastered most of yours." Since many people enjoy talking about themselves, Nicole thought that the compliment gave Isabella an easy way to redirect the conversation.

"Yeah, I have," said Isabella. "But I may have left Randy behind when I did."

Apparently, Isabella wasn't looking for an easy out.

"Through no fault of his own, Randy lost his job soon after we were married. He tried finding another but wasn't having much luck, so I suggested that he run our home. And he does, but I think he hates it. We hardly ever talk about it and … well, I do my part to kill the conversation unintentionally because I always end up crowing about some accomplishment at work."

Degree in counseling or not, Nicole felt like she had to say something. It just needed to be a lot more tactful than the retort that was running through her head—you need to tell Randy to get his head out of his keister because he doesn't know how good he has it. She took a breath. "I need to say again …"

"That you're not a counselor," Isabella said, finishing Nicole's disclaimer for her.

"Sorry. I don't mean to sound like a broken record, but in my position, it's an important distinction. And in this case, it's even more important because I'm not a marriage counselor. I'm not even married. But assuming that it's the role reversal that's got him down, it doesn't sound like anything you can't solve. He had plans and dreams when you were first married, right?"

"Yeah, he was a first-level manager for customer support at a national shipping company. He thought he had a clear path to upper management until they automated much of what his subordinates did. And then, suddenly, they didn't need him."

"Well, if management is his thing …" Nicole said slowly as she considered the implications. "You would undoubtedly know better than me, but aren't jobs requiring interpersonal skills, like sales, still on the upswing?"

"Upswing?" said Isabella. "I'm not sure about that but they are at least stable." She laughed once softly. "I suppose if Eliza turns out to be outrageously successful and we use her to understand the potential customer, AI might take on that job, too, but that's not going to be anytime soon. Well, I don't think it would be soon anyway."

"So, maybe not sales. Did he have any other interests that might turn into a career?"

Isabella slid back in her chair, a hand coming up to slap her forehead with the palm of her hand. "I can't believe I didn't think of this earlier, but Randy used to mention human resources as an area he thought he'd like. And talk about a job that relies on human interaction and interpersonal skills!" Isabella was quiet a moment, then continued more thoughtfully. "He talked about it before we were married, but I doubt anything has changed. Seems like it might work."

"It's worth a try," said Nicole. "So, if it was me, I'd take a few days off work and take him some place that's meaningful for the two of you so you can work out the details of your new partnership." She thought about suggesting that the two of them see a marriage counselor first but figured Isabella would just think she was being extremely careful. And she was. But she also had first-hand experience in how quickly and dramatically life could change. She didn't say anything, however, because, in the end, Isabella would do what she thought best.

"You don't know how many times I've had a similar thought," said Isabella. "But it was always, I'll do it as soon as I reached the next big milestone at work. Pretty soon, all the milestones added up to three years. That, however, ends Friday morning when I leave here. I even know where we'll go. Randy hasn't mentioned the spot in years, but he found a quiet place where he liked to hike. We'll go there."

"Sounds perfect," said Nicole. "Where is it?"

"I've only been there once, but it's somewhere beyond Geneva Lake toward the Maroon Bells-Snowmass Wilderness."

THURSDAY, MAY 8

Morning, Jen's Place

At the sound of a knock on her door, Nicole looked up from the pile of paperwork spread across her desk. "Come in," she called.

The door opened and Isabella stepped in. "Sorry to bother you, but I'm going to have to leave this morning."

"Nothing wrong, I hope."

"Wrong, yes, but just how bad it is, I'm not sure. Someone broke into our lab last night and trashed the place. The break-in probably wouldn't have been discovered until Friday, but the president of the company spotted a light in the lab and found the place in shambles. He said all the hardware was smashed and the documentation was scattered all over the room. I'm just waiting for a text from him saying that the Crime Scene Investigator is there since they probably won't let me touch anything until they have a look anyway."

"You want to have a seat while you wait?"

"I don't want to interrupt," Isabella said, waving a hand at the cluttered desk.

"Please do. I could use the break."

Isabella nodded, came in, and sat.

"So, did they catch the person who tore up your lab?" asked Nicole.

"Not yet, and depending on how thorough they were, we could be out a lot of work. Calvin—that's Calvin Whitmer, our programmer—he backs up everything, of course. If whoever did this got to the backups, then ... well, it won't take as long to re-build Eliza a second time, but it might take a year or more to get back to where we were. There's also the chance that all the mess they made was just a cover for something even more malicious. Maybe they planted a trojan in our software?"

That possibility didn't make sense to Nicole. "If someone wanted to plant a trojan that would be activated later, wouldn't they have done so quietly? It seems like by vandalizing your lab, the bad guy put your team on alert for anything in the code that doesn't belong there."

Isabella chuckled, her first departure from the gloom that had surrounded her since entering Nicole's room. "And there goes my career as a detective. You're right. I'm already planning to tell Calvin he has to go through Eliza line by line if there is any chance the intruder got to the backups. That is, assuming we can find him."

"Your programmer is missing?"

"It's only been a couple of days, but yeah, we don't know exactly where he went after ... after Molly committed suicide. There, I said it. That's the violence that I'm hiding from."

"You're not hiding," said Nicole. "It takes time to find the right coping mechanisms for anyone to deal with the shock of violence. And that's why you're here, to start that search."

"Well, hopefully, the search doesn't have to be uninterrupted because I've got to get back to the lab today." Isabella glanced at her phone. "Sorry. I thought I felt a vibration, but it was nothing. Probably just me shaking."

"Look. In a few days when things settle down, why don't you come back and finish your stay? I'm sure Josey will have some tasty meals planned and you can chill on the back deck, enjoy the sunrises and sunsets, or hit some of the hiking or biking trails nearby. It'll help with the shakes."

"Thanks, I will. If nothing else, can I drop by for dinner sometime? I really enjoyed our talk last night."

"I did, too. Drop by whenever you have time."

Nicole found herself idly twisting a strand of her hair around a finger, a mannerism that tended to accompany being lost in thought. And true to form, her thoughts had moved on from the question about dinner almost before she had answered it. "Not to be an armchair detective or anything, but do you think that the break-in at your lab and your missing programmer could be related?"

"That idea has crossed my mind," admitted Isabella. "Apparently, there are no obvious signs of forced entry at the lab, although a closer look by the police may turn up something yet. But, if it's an inside job, there's not many other people to suspect. Besides the three of us on the team, there's only a handful of others who had access to it. Hopefully, whoever comes out to process the scene will find some fingerprints that don't belong."

"Well, if you're lucky enough to get Brien Clarke as the Crime Scene Investigator, you can tell him I said hi."

"Another of your friends?" asked Isabella.

"He's the boyfriend of the private investigator next door."

"I think the PI came over to the shelter last night after you went up to your room. I was sitting near a fireplace in one of the common areas and she came in with a coffee or tea. At least, that was what one of your guests told me. She's a tall blonde, right?"

"That could be her," replied Nicole. "But don't be misled by appearances. She's FBI-trained and a lot tougher than she looks. And if the police strike out finding Calvin, I understand she works missing persons cases from time to time."

"Well, I hope it doesn't come to that," said Isabella, flinching just as she finished the statement. "That vibration definitely wasn't my imagination."

She raised the phone to her eyes. After a moment, she released a long sigh.

"It looks like I'm going to be shut out of the lab for most or all of the day, but my boss would like me to come in anyway. The police are already asking him questions about Calvin that he can't answer."

FRIDAY, MAY 9

Evening, The Huttons' Apartment

*O**h, Randy?* came the all too familiar voice from inside his head.

"Where the hell have you been?" the man asked as he stabbed the air with a finger that he couldn't point at anyone.

Easy there, buckeroo. It was only Wednesday morning when we talked about wrecking the lab.

"Easy for you to say, buckeroo, because I was the one taking all the risks. And what do you do? You don't even take a moment to thank me? Way to go, Randy. You've saved mankind from wandering aimlessly in a meaningless world."

Is that what you think you did?

"Well, yeah," Randy replied slowly, his bravado faltering with Schumann's pointed question. "According to you, the distrust between the working man and the machines that would take their place will remain because there will be no Eliza to force her misinformation on them."

So, I did. But then, I wasn't expecting you to be such an advocate. I suppose wrecking that bitch's lab must have felt pretty good.

"Now, wait a second. Isabella's no ... She's ..." Randy's voice trailed off each time he tried to refute Schumann's assertion, and he knew why. The consistency between his feelings and Schumann's words brought an unease that was buried just below the surface to the center of his thoughts. It was true that he had enjoyed destroying her lab. Each computer he smashed was a blow against the shipping company that had placed profit above his livelihood. Each camera he demolished chipped away at the falsehoods Isabella secretly harbored against him. Each microphone he destroyed was another precious day he had given mankind to respond to the threat of artificial intelligence. Schumann had been right. He was in a fight for humanity. The war against AI was giving him a sense of self-satisfaction.

"Yeah. Isabella is in the middle of this mess. But with the extra time I've given the government, they'll recognize that the greedy corporate heads only see dollar signs when they see AI, not the way it will gut the common working man. That senator from Nevada—he seems like the kind of guy who'd love nothing better than to apply the brakes to AI development, what with his experience with that crazy military drone."

Perhaps you're right, said Schumann softly.

Randy started to relax. For as long as he had heard Schumann in his head, the voice had never agreed with him on anything. Maybe they were turning a corner.

Perhaps you're right that I should have talked to the Nevada Senator because you are the most useless, pathetic excuse for a man that I've ever met.

"What are you talking about? I destroyed her lab. I've given the government some time to recognize that they're playing with fire."

Hardly. You destroyed some laptops and peripherals, which can be easily replaced. Several have been already. And you tore the documentation out of the binders and scattered the pages around the room, but they didn't even bother picking that up. They just swept up the paper and printed out a new copy. And the software? You didn't even touch it, so all they have to do is reload it when the hardware is ready. It's only been two days and they're nearly operational already. You've got to be the biggest screw-up I've ever had the displeasure of knowing.

"But ... But ..."

So, now you can't even talk without stammering? Why the hell did I ever think you were anything other than the useless piece of excrement that your wife thinks you are.

"Hold on. Yeah, her opinion of me isn't the greatest, but ..."

But what? But you have her fooled? Spare me. She only keeps you around because she's not sure what a divorce would do to her business. Yeah, her business of making you and your kind obsolete is a helluva lot more important to her than you or your cronies. She'll be one of the rich ruling elite, and you? Well, if you're lucky, you'll be dead. But then, you're never lucky. You'll just be taking your meals out of a trash dumpster downtown.

"I can't believe she knows ..."

Again, Randy's voice trailed off, but this time it was because he could think of no way to argue with the voice. Of course, Isabella valued her work more than him. She paid the bills while he only added to the balance due. Of those facts, she was well aware.

"OK," he said after a moment as he massaged his temples with his fingertips. "I suppose they store the software on a server somewhere. Maybe I can find out where and destroy it?"

Figured out that the software is on a server somewhere all by yourself, did you, Einstein? And are you thinking that they have the backups on the same system? Moron! Look, the door to setting them back by destroying the software has closed. Breakthrough Systems is not going to be so lax with security next time.

"But we can't just sit by and let them win," said Randy.

Who said anything about conceding? Fortunately, another window to slow them down has opened. Do you know the name Calvin Whitmer?

"That programmer who disappeared after that woman died?"

Still don't know Molly's name, do you? But at least you know Calvin, the software engineer behind Eliza. The police found and cleared him. He was in a bar up in the foothills. Several people saw him there at the time you were breaking into the lab. Your wife talked him into coming back, so if you stop him, mankind will get a temporary reprieve.

"Stop him?" said Randy, a frown spreading over his face. "How would I do that?"

Oh, I don't know. Maybe break all his fingers? No, wait. He could still explain all his code to your wife and you know how fast she types. So, you'll have to cut out his tongue, too.

Randy's head was slowly shaking. He knew he could handle the up-close-and-personal type of violence that Schumann was describing. After all, he had a history, albeit one that hadn't yet involved humans. But even if he did what Schumann asked, all the programmer would have to do was type his name with an elbow, and he'd end up in prison. He was going to tell Schumann as much when the voice continued.

Or you could just kill him.

"You can't be serious. I don't own a gun. I don't even know how to use one."

Oh, I'm deadly serious, replied Schumann. And who said anything about a gun? I know that's not your thing. No, you're the kind that likes to watch as the flames devour the flesh of your prey.

"I ... How ... You couldn't ..." Randy stammered.

How did I know you wet your bed until you were twelve? asked Schumann. How did I know your mother beat you and locked you in a closet with the damp sheets each day afterward? How did I know that you finally found solace in stealing your neighbors' dogs and burning them alive? I could tell you that you talk in your sleep, which you do. But I know because ... I'm you.

"But it's been twenty years. All that is behind me."

It's been seventeen and it's not behind you, replied Schumann. It won't be behind you until you settle your accounts with life.

"I don't owe anyone anything."

Schumann laughed. It was the cruelest, most merciless laugh Randy had ever heard.

Do you think it's just part of the normal course of events that you're still alive? Well, it isn't. Your mother found out about the third dog you killed, and she was coming home from work early to deal with you. You'd considered that possibility and decided to throw yourself on her mercy. The trouble with that strategy, however, is that she has none. She's more of an eye-for-an-eye kind of person ... not that she would have killed you. But with what she had planned, you might have preferred death.

Randy recognized his thought about begging for his mother's compassion. He also recalled his fear that it wouldn't work, which Schumann now confirmed.

She was going to confront you, not so you could talk her out of her plan, but so you would know that she could no longer be associated with such a disappointing human, Schumann said. And this time, she was going to leave scars that no one would ever see, save perhaps the undertaker.

It wasn't difficult for Randy to believe the voice's words. His mother tended to deal with life's setbacks by destroying all evidence that anything had ever been wrong. She had eradicated every indication that his father had ever existed even though Randy had been desperate to save a few reminders of him—a picture, a note, a birthday gift. But she had disposed of them all, so now, with the image of his father faded from his memory, she had succeeded in destroying the man completely.

But fortunately, destiny had a different fate in mind for you, said Schumann. It's a fate that, if you don't mess it up, involves the saving of mankind. You'll be a god among men.

You see, your mother crashed her car in her blind rage on the drive home. She could hardly deal with your despicable ways with her arm in a sling, so you were banished to your grandparents. Her plan was to have you return home once her arm healed, but once again, your calling interceded on your behalf. It allowed you to remain on the farm until she felt you could pull your own weight. So, now you owe. You owe destiny for all it's done for you.

His exile to the farm was just another case of his mother destroying the evidence of a problem except this time, he was the thorn in her side. With him gone, her perfect order would be restored, and she could act like nothing had ever been amiss. Then, when he was old enough to work a menial job, she'd have him back so she could help herself to his meager pay. It was, as she put it, "a mere pittance" toward what he owed her.

Randy could see no point in trying to argue with Schumann because he knew the voice was right. "OK," he said. "What do I have to do?"

Nothing that you'll find distasteful. Calvin just inherited a house from an uncle. It's just a shack up in the foothills, but he has grand plans for it. It's currently loaded with chemicals for stripping paint and for repainting and staining. It'll go up like a box of tinder and no one will be the wiser. You just need to make sure he doesn't get out before the flames have a chance to do their work.

"Now hold ..." Randy got no further because Schumann was gone. He could feel it. Now, he just wondered how many nightmare-filled evenings it would take before he gave in to exhaustion and killed Calvin Whitmer.

But even as the question came to his mind, he realized that wasn't going to be a problem. Schumann's words were reverberating through his psyche. Already, he was starting to look forward to being a god among men, the divine being that had saved the world from artificial intelligence.

THURSDAY, MAY 15

Evening, Jen's Place

Nicole saw Isabella enter the Jen's Place dining room. She waved a hand toward the buffet line and then went to meet her in the serving area. "It's lasagna night," said Nicole. "It's best we dig in now because this dish goes really fast."

"You've sold me," said Isabella.

After the women had filled their plates with pasta, salad, and a roll, they moved to a table near the back of the room. "So, how are you doing?" asked Nicole as the women sat.

"OK," was Isabella's one-word response. Nicole knew there was more but didn't want to pry. But before she could move the conversation to a new topic, Isabella said, "I feel so bad about Molly, like I should have been there for her more than I was. But her suicide just came out of the blue."

Nicole didn't immediately recall the name, Molly, until Isabella said "suicide" and then, everything fell into place including a rejoinder. "Whoa, hold on. The last thing you should be doing is taking on responsibility where it's not called for. You're working on a cutting-edge technology that has caught the eye of a big tech company, and so, your job has been expanding at the speed of light. You have a team looking to you for direction. And you have a husband who perhaps feels a bit left behind. I think that's more than enough on your plate already."

"Well, that's because you don't know the whole story," replied Isabella. "When Molly killed herself, she said it was because I hadn't returned her feelings."

"OK," Nicole said slowly. "And now that I know, it doesn't make any difference." Isabella had put a bite of lasagna on her fork but put it back on the plate without a taste.

"Look," continued Nicole. "You said Molly's suicide came out of the blue. You can't be expected to read someone else's mind."

"I know," she replied, as she stared at the plate of untouched food in front of her. "And it wasn't like I gave her any reason to expect anything more from me ... at least that I can think of. And I've given it a lot of thought. But maybe that was the problem. Maybe if I had paid more attention to her, it wouldn't have happened."

"So, Molly never approached you to say she had feelings toward you?"

"No. I couldn't have missed that."

"And as far as you know, she never sought help anywhere else? Parents? Counselors?"

"Not her parents," said Isabella. "I've talked to them. They were as shattered by the news as everyone else."

"So, what happened was tragic. There's no denying that. But don't you think it's time to cut yourself some slack?"

Isabella nodded, saying, "I suppose so."

"Good." Nicole knew it wouldn't be as simple as getting Isabella to admit she was beating herself up over something she couldn't control, but it was a start in her opinion.

Finally, Isabella picked up her fork and took a taste of the lasagna. "Oh, my, you weren't kidding," she said. "This is really good."

Nicole nodded knowingly. She was certain Josey's lasagna was really therapeutic, but Isabella wouldn't be the first to forget about her cares for a time while dining on it. "I'm glad you could come by so soon after the break-in at your lab."

"Me, too," replied Isabella, pausing to take a nibble of her roll before another mouthful of pasta. "It could have been much worse, but fortunately, the vandal only destroyed some hardware. Insurance paid for most of that, although we took the opportunity to upgrade our systems a bit. Those expenditures have added to our pressure to perform, but nothing we can't handle."

"You're sure not wasting any time," replied Nicole.

"Well, you gotta strike while the iron's hot."

Nicole wasn't sure that the platitude fit, and perhaps her uncertainty showed as Isabella said, "I guess it's not a problem telling you this, but the cloud from the destruction of our lab had a silver lining. We got a second big tech company interested in Eliza because of it."

Nicole laughed. "Do you always talk in clichés?"

Isabella shrugged. "I guess if the shoe fits ..." she said deadpan, then grinned. "Anyway, we have a second potential user who could be worth millions if Eliza performs the way I know she can. Even Randy's onboard with this new development."

"So, the getaway to the mountains to plan his transition to human resources got Randy excited, did it?"

Isabella finished a bite of her salad before she answered, but her head was shaking before she spoke, and a frown was forming on her face. "Unfortunately, no, but only because I haven't had a chance to bring it up with everything that has happened. But I will as soon as he gets back."

The last thing Nicole wanted to do was to spoil Isabella's improving mood, so she said, "But your husband's already involved?"

Isabella's smile returned. "He is. When I told him about this new opportunity, I mentioned that my team and I would probably have to rent some space for a couple of days until all the new systems were fully integrated and tested. He asked if I wanted to use our place."

Isabella seemed intent on building the perfect bite of meat, sauce, and noodles before popping them into her mouth. But after swallowing it, she said, "Frankly, I wasn't ready for his offer. But after I hemmed and hawed for a few seconds, some of it apparently coming across as a yes, he said he'd be happy to spend a couple of days up in the mountains."

"That was nice of him," Nicole replied, although she thought it seemed a bit more selfish than selfless. Sure, Isabella's team's discussion of modeling people's behavior to make AI a better teammate would bore him—or go over his head—but couldn't he at least stay around and help her with hosting the group? She took a bite of her lasagna, hoping it would cover her lukewarm feelings.

Perhaps, it did, as Isabella said, "Yes, it was nice. We'll save some money, and I won't have to worry that we're talking too loudly or working too late." She frowned. "And, frankly, Randy hasn't slept that well for ... well, at least a year now."

Nicole thought that the loss of his customer service job almost had to be a contributing factor to his sleep issues and probably, the primary one. But she avoided offering unqualified opinions because she heard too many during her days working in biomedical engineering—"the doctor's office should just read my blood pressure off my fitness watch instead of all that rigmarole they do." So, instead, she said, "That must have been a tough time for both of you."

Isabella tilted her head in something of a shrug. "It was. But Randy's symptoms were minor—poor appetite, irritability, hearing voices, lethargy, and lack of sleep. Our doctor said that these are rather common symptoms of male depression, and Randy certainly had reason to be depressed with what his company had done to him."

Apparently, Nicole wasn't the only one thinking that Randy's termination was probably a precipitating factor in his loss of sleep, but other parts of Isabella's statement didn't fit Nicole's emerging picture of the situation nearly as well. "Your doctor said that hearing voices was typical of depression?"

Because biomedical engineering had a continuously expanding role in the treatment of depression, with devices that used everything from low frequency, weak magnetic signals to the strong shocks used in electroconvulsive therapy, Nicole knew a considerable amount about the condition. And that knowledge made her wonder about the auditory hallucinations, which tended to occur primarily in cases of severe or psychotic depression.

Isabella's brow knitted in concentration as she chewed a bite of her roll followed by a forkful of lasagna. After a moment, she released a long sigh. "Maybe, but I'm thinking that the voices thing came up later, sometime after he went to see our doctor. But even at the time, Randy said he wasn't sure he had heard anything. And it hasn't happened since."

She paused. "Personally, I wondered if he was just catching a few words from Eliza coming from a speaker in a different room, but that wasn't the case. Randy said if he heard anything, it was a man's voice, not a woman's."

That all sounded innocent enough—if anything connected with hearing voices could be considered such—but Nicole was still wondering if there was an underlying problem. "Before his job ended at the shipping company, did he have any history of depression?"

Isabella laughed. "Just the opposite. He was always clowning around, the proverbial life of the party." Her grin disappeared. "Why did you want to know that?"

"Oh, it's probably nothing. It's just that most everyone is familiar with poor sleep and poor appetite when they're worried about something, but hearing voices? Not so much. If it comes back, you may want to get a professional opinion."

"Oh, I would. If he starts talking to Harvey, I'll have all kinds of questions for the docs," Isabella said with a smile.

Nicole wasn't sure she knew what Isabella meant but took a guess. "Harvey? Are you talking about that old movie with the invisible rabbit?"

"Correct. I guess Randy wasn't the only one losing sleep. I probably stayed up till two in the morning watching that one," Isabella replied.

"Anyway, maybe the best thing about Randy getting out of our apartment for a few days is that he gets some time away from the place—he hardly ever goes anywhere. And while everyone has a link to Eliza on their phone, if we work at our apartment, she has all the microphones and cameras she's used to, and she can help us come up with the pitch for our potential new customer. We're sure not going to find that kind of assistance in any hotel room or rented office space."

"That's right. You mentioned that you'd installed Eliza at work and at your apartment so you could get some data about its performance." Nicole paused, a concern she had not considered previously coming to mind. "Are you at all concerned about using yourself and your team as part of your research? I mean, self-experimentation has resulted in some pretty sordid situations."

"Don't you plug yourself into every piece of biomedical equipment you design?" Isabella asked, again in her deadpan tone of voice.

Nicole chuckled. "I'm a little big for the monitoring systems I've been working on for premature babies."

Isabella seemed to hurry a mouthful of food down her throat, then let her jaw drop for effect. Nicole almost laughed aloud.

"Monitoring preemies? You gotta tell me more. But I'll answer your question first. If the data we're collecting was the final validation and safety analysis, then yes, I'd be extremely worried about what we're doing. But it's not. It's just formative evaluations that let us make subtle course corrections as we go along. Some of it's pretty obvious, like asking people how they are feeling to help Eliza hone her skill at recognizing human emotions. But some are less intrusive, like observing how my team reacts to her suggestions. Do they follow her ideas, or do they continue doing what they were doing?"

Nicole pondered Isabella's response for a moment. "So, it's like the example you gave about a sound being almost too soft for a human to hear, in which case, Eliza might recommend that the person try the test again and get closer? If they do, then Eliza probably predicted the person's hearing vulnerability correctly."

"With the emphasis on probably," Isabella replied. "Seldom are the trends we see in our team data so clearcut that there aren't several possibilities." She flinched slightly, then pulled a phone from a pocket and checked the display.

"Sorry," said Isabella. "That was a text from Randy. Anyway, Calvin, our programmer, wanted to call this test the 'Reverse Turing Test' because he believes it's a ground-breaking concept. I've had a hard time convincing him that first, the name is confusing—the Turing test deals with whether people can distinguish between a computer and a human just by asking questions. So, a reverse Turing sounds like Eliza is trying to distinguish humans from a computer ... or something like that, which she isn't. We just want to see if people follow her advice. And, second, I've told him that formative evaluation during development is nothing new."

"Well, at least he's excited about the work he's doing," said Nicole.

"I might call it overexaggerating his contributions, but yeah, he's excited. But enough on my team and our tribulations. Tell me more about your systems to monitor premature babies. That's got to be fascinating stuff."

"I'm not sure that would be the general public's consensus, but yeah, I think so." With that, Nicole launched into a summary that kept them occupied through dinner.

When they finished the meal, Isabella said, "I can't believe how much I've enjoyed this evening. It's not often I find anyone as interested in technology and research as me."

"Ditto," said Nicole.

"Look, that text from Randy was a little vague about when he'd return from hiking—something between Saturday night and Tuesday. But knowing him, it'll be Tuesday. I know we just finished dinner, but would you be interested in doing it again on Monday night? But on

Monday, it's my treat someplace other than Jen's Place. I've freeloaded enough from here."

"I'm not sure you've even finished your original stay," said Nicole.

"I'm pretty sure with as much as I ate tonight, my stay is complete. So, I'll text you the location of the restaurant tomorrow after I make the reservation. Any kind of food you don't like?"

"I eat just about anything," replied Nicole.

"Then, it'll probably be Chinese. I know a great place." Isabella left to prepare her apartment for tomorrow's planning session. Unfortunately, that meant Nicole had no excuse to avoid the mountain of paperwork that seemed to be a permanent fixture on her desk.

SATURDAY, MAY 17

Late Morning, The Huttons' Apartment

"B ev?" said Isabella as she opened her front door to find Randy's mother standing there. "I didn't expect to see you out here." Isabella stepped forward and the two women embraced.

"I'm sorry to drop in unannounced, but an old friend in Great Bend died and I'm headed there now." Bev paused to shake her head. "Guess I have a lot more of that to look forward to in my old age. Anyway, I just found out last night, and I didn't want to call and disturb you two."

"Our door is always open to you," replied Isabella.

At that moment, the discussion of an idea that Isabella, Julia, and Calvin had been considering heated up and Isabella could hear the voices of her team coming from the living area. Apparently, Bev did, too. "Is Randy back there?"

"No, sorry. He went out of town for a couple of days, up hiking in the mountains. He won't be back until ... well, probably Tuesday. That's just my work team you're hearing. But come on in. The coffee's made and we were about to order some sub sandwiches for lunch."

"I don't want to interrupt."

"You're not," said Isabella.

"You've got your team at your apartment on a Saturday, they're arguing passionately about their ideas, and I'm not interrupting anything?"

"Not at all. They just think better at the top of their lungs," replied Isabella with a smirk. "Now, come on in, and let's see what everyone wants to eat." Bev still seemed to be hesitating, so Isabella took her hand and pulled her through the open door.

"Well, if you insist," Bev said with a laugh. "And if the coffee's made ..."

"It is." They went into the kitchen where Isabella poured both of them a cup. "So, if you've driven in from Casper this morning, you can probably use this."

"I can, although this isn't my first caffeine break." Bev took a sip. "Delicious as always." She set the cup down on the kitchen island, then sat on one of the stools around it. She took a breath as if preparing to say something, but then stopped. Then, the pattern repeated, although this time she spoke. "You've made me feel better already. From three hundred miles away, I had the impression that Randy never left the apartment. So, to find him off hiking, well, that can only be a change for the good."

"I hope so. Say, did Randy ever talk about working in human resources that you can remember?"

Bev took another sip of coffee, then rubbed her chin with a hand as she stared across the room. "Yeah, from time to time, he did," she said, looking back at Isabella. "Are you thinking that's a way for him to get back into the workforce?"

"I am. I'm thinking that HR will be an area where human-to-human interaction will be key for some time yet, so I and the technology I'm working on won't be the enemy anymore."

"Don't be ridiculous," said Bev. "You aren't the enemy. I don't understand everything you do, but I'm pretty sure if you weren't doing it, someone else would be. And that being the case, it's better that you're doing it and putting food on the table."

Isabella suspected that Bev was right in thinking this was a logical next step for AI at work. But what she was less sure about was whether the bridge she was building between man and machine would be the stable commodity that she hoped. Or would AI evolve to the point where understanding a human counterpart was immaterial because humans were irrelevant? That outcome certainly seemed possible. For now, however, she put those concerns aside. She had to take advantage of where they were in the development of intelligent systems, which meant developing Eliza. And in turn, she'd help get Randy back on his feet, doing something he enjoyed more than running their home.

"I've been checking on some of the schools around here, and with some economizing, we can get him into an HR-related degree program. And though it's not directly related, his work in customer service management should help, too."

"I wish I could help ..."

Isabella stopped her with the wave of a hand before Bev had time to say more. Her husband had died when Randy was little, and she had been forced out of retirement to return to teaching third grade. She'd even had Randy go stay with his grandparents for a couple of weeks while she renewed her teaching certificate. But while that sacrifice had allowed her to keep her home, she was living paycheck to paycheck and couldn't afford to help with her son's educational expenses.

"We'll be fine. Say, when do you expect to get back home from the funeral?"

"Tuesday."

"If you want to stick around Denver, he should be coming home about then?"

Bev paused a moment. "Sorry, but I'll be ready to get back to my own home by then. You know how it is. Maybe next time?"

"Anytime. And I'll have Randy give you a call when he gets back."

"That would be great. I've called him a few times over the last six months or so, but he's never called back."

Isabella was preparing to take a sip of her coffee but nearly dropped her cup at these words. "What?"

"Don't be mad at him," Bev said. "He doesn't need guilt to deal with on top of everything else he has weighing him down."

Isabella was certain she didn't agree—Bev was a little too understanding where her son was concerned—but she knew there was no point trying to debate the matter with her. So, she simply said, "Trust me, he'll call this time."

"And I'd love to hear from him."

"Well, I think I better go take lunch orders or I'm going to have a revolt on my hands." The women stood and walked into the living room.

"Bev, this is Julia and Calvin," said Isabella, extending a hand toward each of the others as she said their names. "And guys, this is Beverly. Beverly Hutton, Randy's mom."

Late Evening, The Foothills West of Denver

"Where the hell is he?" Randy muttered to himself. He knew that Calvin, the team's programmer, had been part of the group that was meeting at his apartment, but they should have finished hours ago. What could he be doing?

That question brought so many images into his thoughts that he slapped the palm of a hand against his head as if trying to dislodge them. Featured among them was Calvin and his wife in bed together, which was necessarily vague since he'd never met the man. That fact, however, seemed no obstacle to his mind's eye, which just made the vision of his wife's naked body that much clearer. They were "going at it" in the comfort of her bed while he was out here, freezing his butt off behind Calvin's cabin.

Perhaps these images were just fantasy, Randy thought. Schumann had never said Isabella was fooling around, and he seemed to know about all the comings and goings at work. But then again, maybe she had hidden her promiscuity from Schumann. After all, it wasn't like she and Calvin would be copulating on the table in the Breakthrough Systems lunchroom.

He felt like these images should infuriate him, but strangely, they didn't. It was more just the mental loop of her fumbling and fiddling with another man over and over that was pushing him to the brink. He needed to think of better times, and other situations, and the one that came unbidden into his thoughts was the last dog he had killed. Unlike the vague picture of Calvin, these images were as clear in his mind as if they had happened yesterday.

Schumann seemed to believe that Randy should relish all parts of the memories of the dogs he had tortured and killed, but he didn't. He didn't like the dog's howls of terror, its shrieks of pain. He only endured them because, in the end, the look of ... he didn't know what to call it? Rapture? A transition to a different plane of existence? He only found it in the dog's eyes, but whatever it was, it was a look like none other he had ever witnessed. And, frankly, he had stumbled onto it by accident.

He had killed the first dog out of spite; his neighbor had called his mother a whore. Perhaps if he knew then what he knew now, the comment wouldn't have bothered him. But he was just a kid, and the dog was the neighbor's prized possession. So, he had suffered through the stench of burning fur and the howls of agony only to be completely mesmerized by the look in the canine's eyes during the final moments. In the dog's transition from living to dead, Randy had found a moment of bliss in his otherwise tormented existence.

A week later, the memory had faded. Randy was no longer sure he had seen or felt anything. That mystery, however, was easily solved. When he killed the second dog, his experience was not the same; it was even better. He knew he wouldn't stop.

Two weeks after that a third opportunity presented itself. Randy knew he hadn't waited long enough. In his quiet neighborhood on the outskirts of Casper, people were still whispering about a couple of missing pets. The blame, however, was being placed on two coyotes who, amid a drought that was making game scarce, had been testing the boundaries of the town for several weeks. No one thought they had a serial killer in training in their midst.

His impatience, however, proved his downfall. Someone saw him luring the dog away from its yard and called his mother. He completed the deed and returned home not knowing how close he had come to being a witness to his own torture at his mother's hands. But as Schumann had said, fate had a different plan for him.

Randy stood up from his hiding spot in the woods just behind the cabin. He was sore from his exertions earlier in the day and his muscles were starting to cramp. As it was a night with a nearly full moon, the movement would have been risky if Calvin had neighbors, but fortunately for Randy, the nearest house was close to a half-mile away.

Knowing that Calvin was busy at his apartment earlier in the day, Randy had broken into his shack just after noon. It had been laughably easy, but then, there was little inside worth stealing. Since the success of this ritual rested on his ability to look the man in the eye as death overtook him, his trap had to be set carefully and precisely. It had taken him nearly four hours to build it, but in the end, he had little doubt it would work. That was because none of it relied on automation—no sensors, no phones, no wireless feeds, not even a physical tripwire. Rather, it was as it should be—human-operated.

First, he would draw the man to one of the windows in the back of the property. That distraction was easily implemented by a small torch placed just beyond the glass. He would light it and the man would be drawn to the window like a moth to a flame. "Moth to a flame," Randy muttered. "Or maybe, man to a flame?" He smiled at his cleverness.

Then, when he saw his victim at the window, Randy would pull a rope that allowed a heavy object to swing down from the ceiling and pin Calvin to the back wall of the cabin. That, of course, was the crucial step, and he had been concerned on the drive up that he wouldn't find the materials he needed. So, he had brought a set of door hinges, some boards, and a few tools with him in the trunk of his car. The rest of what he needed—something with more weight than a bit of lumber—became apparent as soon as he was inside the cabin. Someone, perhaps Calvin himself, was in the process of rebuilding a stone fireplace. He could simply lash some of the stones to a wooden frame—one that he was now calling the door to Hades in his mind. The door would even fit close enough to the ceiling that it would be lost in the shadows of the night.

Perfecting the operation of Hades's door took Randy the bulk of the time, but after experimenting with two or three stones, he had it working consistently. Only then did he load the wooden framework with the eight stones he had selected for his trap. Clearly, that number had enough weight to stun his prey and knock the air from his lungs, but hopefully, Calvin wouldn't be left unconscious; that might ruin everything.

Next, Randy stuffed some rags and small pieces of wood between the larger stones and soaked everything in kerosene. As Schumann had said, there were enough chemicals in the shack—varnish, paint thinner, paint stripper, and the like—that Calvin would never notice the additional smell. Finally, with his prey pinned helplessly to the back wall, Randy would light the fire using a rag soaked in kerosene and pushed through a hole he had cut.

Randy figured his prey might still have the strength to thrash around enough to break the window, but for his purposes, that was actually better. Although he didn't think the mystical connection that he felt to a departing spirit would be affected by glass, a shattered pane would eliminate even that slim possibility. He'd even considered videotaping the entire ritual, but if one layer of glass was worrisome, lights and video equipment pushed his mind toward panic. Instead, he'd watch with his unaided eye while holding his phone to the side to capture the event. If anything in the process of recording the man's death was spoiled by the technology, at least he'd have the memory to cherish for the rest of his life. Or rather, he'd have it until the images faded from his mind and he needed another "fix."

Randy checked his phone. It was late, much later than he'd expected, and he started thinking that the programmer was staying in town tonight to avoid the return drive in the morning. So, he decided to take shelter in his car. It would be an uncomfortable night, but a little lost sleep was preferable to his prey stumbling upon the trap when he was sleeping in a motel. And the way his car was parked just down the road, he was sure an approaching car's headlights would wake him.

But just as he decided to leave, he saw headlights approaching. The car parked in the short gravel turnout for the cabin, and a man exited. Although there seemed no reason for anyone other than Calvin to be at this remote location in the middle of the night, any lingering doubt that Randy might have felt about the man's identity disappeared when the moonlight illuminated the white logo of Breakthrough Systems on the notebook he carried.

His prey walked slowly toward the cabin, shuffling his feet and stumbling a couple of times. He sat down heavily at a picnic table in the front yard, setting a glass on the tabletop. Having seen the inside of the cabin, Randy figured Calvin probably took most of his meals out here as it was one of the only rooms he had ever seen that rivaled his bedroom for filthiness.

Perhaps it was just the hour, but Randy suspected the man was drunk. That thought, however, unleashed a new worry—what if alcohol blunted the reaction he hoped to observe? He considered following his quarry into the shack, overpowering him, and tying him up until he was sober, but that seemed too risky. For all he knew, Calvin was a black belt in some martial art and he would be the one overpowered. So, he decided to let the ritual play out and hope for the best.

Calvin stumbled into the cabin and immediately collapsed headfirst onto the bed. Had he passed out? Even a burning torch might not get his attention if he had. But after a few moments, the man pulled himself into a sitting position on the edge of the bed. It was time.

Randy lit the torch. At first, the programmer just stared. But after a moment and a vigorous shake of his head, he jumped up and ran across the room. Clearly, Randy's concern about whether his trap would be hidden in the shadows of the ceiling was misplaced; Calvin was so focused on the fire that he ran into a chair before he reached the back wall still clutching a knee.

Randy yanked on the rope that held the framework of boards and stones in place and it came crashing down. Calvin screamed. Randy lit the kerosene-soaked rag and in a moment, flames started licking up the framework of boards and stones.

Calvin screamed again and, as Randy had guessed, started thrashing violently against the weight that had him pinned against the wall. Despite all the injuries his prey must have sustained already—broken bones certainly weren't out of the question—he fought savagely against his constraints. Then, Calvin dropped out of sight, perhaps using his remaining strength and gravity to drop down toward the floor.

The pane of glass in the back window had stubbornly remained unbroken, and Randy pressed his head against it to try to catch a glimpse of his prey. The action, however, was driven by concern rather than thought—what if he missed the man's passing—and Randy burned his cheek on the glass. He pulled back, cursing his blunder. Looking around, he found a rock on the ground, picked it up, and used it to break the glass. But all that accomplished was to let smoke and heat billow out of the opening.

Randy tried to look inside the cabin, but it was no use. The fire was too hot. He waited a few more minutes, assuring himself that Calvin was dead. Then, he hurried off to his waiting car, not wanting to be anywhere in the vicinity when the police and firefighters arrived.

SUNDAY, MAY 18

Afternoon, The Huttons' Apartment

"I know what you're thinking," said Isabella, as she and Julia returned from the kitchen with tea for her and juice for her coworker. "I should have never set a noon start time for today because that just gave Calvin an excuse to go out and get drunk last night."

Julia grimaced slightly. "We don't know that," she said.

"Care to make a bet?"

Julia looked up toward the ceiling as she shook her head. "I'll pass," then took a sip of her juice.

"Well, at least Calvin wasn't all that helpful with this presentation anyway," said Isabella, belatedly realizing she had said the same thing at least twice already this afternoon. "We just finished the chart covering where we got the name, Eliza, and how that system was believed to be sentient even though it was just simple pattern-matching and pre-programmed responses. Do you think that is going into too much detail?"

"Not at all," replied Julia. "A lot of companies will know that we need better communication between man and machine to make these hybrid teams effective. But a lot of those companies will stop at just asking the human if Eliza is helpful, which doesn't prove anything. An emphasis on proving her place on the team is one of the things that distinguishes us from the competitors."

"Well, that's what …" Isabella's reply was interrupted by a knock on the door.

The two women looked at each other, unsure why Calvin would be knocking when he knew the door was supposed to be open. "Let me see who that is," said Isabella.

When she opened the door, a man in a sports coat and open-collar white shirt stood there with a badge holder in his hand. "Isabella Hutton?"

"Yes."

"I'm Detective Robert Sanders of the Bear Lake County Sheriff's office. Do you mind if I ask you a few questions?"

"No, of course not. Would you like to come in?"

"Thanks. This should only take a few minutes."

Isabella turned and started for the living room, then stopped and turned back to the detective. "I have a coworker here, Julia Morton. If you want to talk to me alone, I'm sure she would excuse us for a while."

"Julia Morton?" the detective repeated.

"That's right."

"Actually, I wanted to talk to her, too." He hesitated a moment. "And I suppose there's no reason why I couldn't talk to both of you at the same time."

"Is this about Calvin Whitmer?" Isabella asked, knowing that he was the most likely common denominator for the two women.

"It is."

"Is he …" Isabella stopped. "Sorry. I'll let you talk to both of us so you won't have to repeat yourself."

When the introductions were complete and everyone had a seat, Detective Sanders asked, "You both know Calvin Whitmer, correct?"

"We all work on the same project," Isabella said as Julia nodded her concurrence. "I'm the team lead and Julia and Calvin work for me."

"At Breakthrough Systems?"

"Correct." At first, Isabella was surprised that the detective had that information. But after a moment's reflection, she realized he had probably known that first and tracked them down using that fact. "Is Calvin alright?" she asked.

The detective looked at her, then Julia, and finally, his gaze went back to Isabella. "I'm afraid there's no easy way to tell you this, but Calvin is dead. He died last night in a fire at his cabin."

"Oh, my God," said Julia, a hand coming to her throat.

"That's awful," said Isabella, the words almost catching in her throat. "He's been talking about all the work he's been doing up there, much of it with paints and chemicals, but he said he was being very careful with them. What happened?"

But rather than answering, the detective asked, "Have either of you been to his cabin before?"

Why would the detective want to know that unless Calvin's death didn't appear to be an accident? Isabella's emotions shifted from primarily confusion to unease. She looked at Julia, who shook her head. "No, neither of us," said Isabella.

"Ms. Morton?"

The apparent requirement that Julia answer for herself served to increase Isabella's anxiety even further. Did she need to request a lawyer? Did she need to say that even though she'd never been there, her fingerprints would be all over things he took home from work? But in the end, she just listened.

"No, I've never been there," said Julia.

The detective nodded but didn't expand on his question. Rather, he asked, "Can you tell me a little bit about this project where Mr. Whitmer worked?"

At least this was familiar territory as Isabella had been the face of this project since the beginning. She could probably answer this question in her sleep.

"It's basically a front-end to artificially intelligent systems. For a smart machine to help a human with a job, which is supposed to be one of their primary functions, the machine needs to know what to expect from the person. You don't want it to say, measure resistance between point A and point B if the human doesn't know how to use a multimeter. If it's just going to make assumptions, then it's no better than a written manual. Our product, which we call Eliza, has knowledge of what their human teammate knows and can do, making man and machine work together more efficiently."

The detective rubbed his chin with a hand for a moment. "I'm no expert, but I thought one of the things people worry about with AI is that it'll get too smart and after a while, it won't need the human at all. And I couldn't help but notice that you said that helping people was supposed to be an important job for AI." The detective had put air quotes around the word supposed, a gesture that Isabella wasn't sure she had seen in the last ten years, but it made his point. "So, is this theoretical role for this software a short-term one at best?"

Isabella wasn't sure why Detective Sanders was asking, which caused some of her foreboding to return. But the question was also somewhat technical and more than a little controversial, which put her back into marketing mode. She glanced at Julia, who seemed to shrug, but perhaps it was just her imagination.

"I'm not sure anyone can predict the course or speed of development of artificial intelligence. Clearly, the researchers have been surprised on occasion. But from my place as a nonexpert as well, I would expect Eliza to be a crucial part of a human-machine team for many years to come. Take your job, for instance, detective. Do you think a robot will replace you in a year or two? Or do you think human insight and intuition will be part of catching crooks for quite a while yet?"

The detective nodded, a gesture Isabella now realized meant I heard you, rather than I agree with you. "Your team is pretty small. Does that reflect the emphasis Breakthrough Systems is placing on your project?"

Isabella's merry-go-round of emotions continued, this question eliciting surprise but with an edge. Was he implying that Eliza wasn't important to the company? If so, he was clearly wrong. But in the end, she answered as a team lead would. "We're a little understaffed … No, make that we're very understaffed now with the loss of Calvin. We had a fourth member of the project, but she … well, she committed suicide not long ago."

"When was this?" asked the detective.

"May sixth," Isabella responded, knowing the date by heart.

Detective Sanders frowned as he raised a wrist to check the date on his watch. "Less than two weeks ago?"

"Yes."

"Where did it happen?"

"At work," replied Isabella. Now that she had said it aloud, Isabella cringed internally at the words. It sounded like she was the head of a project that cut one's life expectancy to mere weeks.

To this point, the detective had listened with his hands folded in his lap. But with these revelations, he pulled a small notebook and pen from a pocket. "I'm not the best with names."

"Her name was Molly Reynolds."

"Thanks," he said as he wrote in the notebook. But unless he was printing it in hieroglyphics, he was recording a lot more than just her name. When he was done, he asked, "Anything else happen recently at Breakthrough Systems that I should know about?"

Was this a test wondered Isabella? If she said nothing and he later learned that some guy down a floor had been bragging about his new deer rifle and Calvin had been shot, would he find her silence suspicious? Isabella could feel her face warming as her blood pressure started to climb.

She looked at Julia, who seemed as intimidated by this line of questioning as she felt. Her coworker grimaced and shook her head.

Isabella was tempted to call a halt to this interview and request a lawyer before she implied something she didn't mean. But then, there seemed no reason why she shouldn't repeat what the detective would already know or would easily learn.

"Well, I don't see how it could be related, but our lab was broken into, and much of our hardware was destroyed. That would have been May seventh."

"So, the day after Ms. Reynolds's suicide?"

"Well, yeah, although Molly died in the morning and the break-in was sometime during the night of the following day." Why she had said that, she wasn't sure. It just seemed like she had to answer the detective's questioning look and fill the silence.

"I think that's all the questions I have for now. We'll be in touch."

The abrupt end to the talk once again caught Isabella off guard. Either there was little suspicious in Calvin's death or the more complete picture of recent events that she had painted had pushed the detective's qualms to a level that required a more formal interview. Somehow, with his promise to be in contact, she guessed it was the latter and she felt somewhat overwhelmed by the whole meeting.

Logically, Isabella knew there was no reason she should feel intimidated, but nonetheless, she did. But maybe the detective could ease some of her concerns. "There's nothing to suggest any kind of foul play in Calvin's death, is there?" she asked.

Detective Sanders's gaze went from face to face for a moment. Finally, he said, "It's still very early in our investigation."

MONDAY, MAY 19

"Can I join you?"

Nicole looked up to find Rebecca Marte standing over her. "Of course, although I should warn you, I'm not in the best mood." Rebecca sat down as if she hadn't even heard.

"It's been a while since I've seen you over here," Nicole continued. "But then, I suspect a roomful of people is not that conducive to an intimate dinner with Brien."

"Probably not, but since he's out of town for a training seminar in Boulder, I thought I'd make an appearance. Of course, his absence explains my bad mood. What's your excuse?"

"Your profession," replied Nicole.

"You have something against private investigators?"

"I meant law enforcement in general. I was supposed to have dinner with a new friend, Isabella Hutton, but she called to cancel. She has to work tonight because she spent the bulk of the afternoon being interrogated at a local police station."

"Hmm. An interview that lasts that long doesn't sound trivial. What's the crime?"

"Murder. Well, potentially anyway, although the police never told her exactly how her coworker died."

Rebecca had just taken a bite of her gyro, a sandwich that regularly got Josey accused of being half Greek even if her last name was O'Neill. But in this case, Rebecca nearly choked on it before getting a breath of air. "Murder? And you think a half-day of her time was excessive?"

"I think it's just giving the real criminal a chance to escape."

Rebecca's eyes narrowed. "Are you saying your friend is a suspect in a murder investigation?"

At first, Nicole couldn't see how the PI had arrived at that question, but in retrospect, it wasn't that much of an inferential leap. She was complaining about the police wasting time, and that wouldn't be the case if Isabella was giving them leads about the killer. It was the police insinuating that she was the murderer that was the waste. "As crazy as it seems to me, yes. She may be a suspect."

"You want to give me a thumbnail or just move on to a different topic?" asked Rebecca.

Nicole was tempted to take the latter option, but if she did, she'd be thinking about Isabella's situation all night anyway. So, she summarized the situation as she understood it.

When she finished, Rebecca said, "OK, we have a four-person team working on an AI-related project. I can't say I completely understand what they were doing, but that's OK. And now, two of the four team members are dead—one by suicide and the second under suspicious circumstances. But you don't know what's suspicious in this programmer's death, correct?"

"The detectives didn't tell Isabella anything specific."

"OK," said Rebecca. "But it must be something troubling enough to bring your friend and her coworker in for a couple of interviews. And you say there's nothing that looks unusual about the suicide?"

"Well, that's a tough question," said Nicole as she rubbed the back of her neck with a hand. She could feel the pressure this discussion was exerting on her, although, at this point, she had no plan to turn back. "Is it suspicious if the person who committed suicide said it was because Isabella didn't return her feelings?"

"Possibly," said Rebecca, surprising Nicole with her rapid and seemingly offhand assessment.

"How much money is this AI project worth?" asked Rebecca.

"Tough to know," said Nicole, hesitating a moment to make the mental shift from death to dollars. "They're currently working on a shoestring budget with one customer interested in giving it a try when they're done. And they just got a second potential customer. But if it works the way Isabella thinks it will, it could be worth millions."

Rebecca was quiet for a moment. "I have to admit, I'm not sure what, if anything, trashing your friend's lab has to do with a possible murder or two. It seems like a bit of a stretch to say it was staged just to get a second customer interested, but I suppose that's possible."

"Whoa," said Nicole. "A possible murder or two? If one of those is Molly Reynolds's suicide, I think you're way off base."

"It wouldn't be the first time," said Rebecca. "But bear with me a moment. Let's say that this Eliza, when it's done, is worth a lot of money. That's seems possible, right?"

"Yeah, I suppose," Nicole said. She wasn't, however, feeling any enthusiasm for the direction this conversation was taking. Somehow, she could already see that Rebecca was going to turn the spotlight back on Isabella.

"OK. Now, let's say Isabella saw some vulnerability in Molly. You said that Molly practically lived at work, that pleasing Isabella was her primary goal in life."

"I didn't say that," replied Nicole, crossing her arms over her chest. But realizing what her body language was saying, she uncrossed them and let them drop to her sides.

"Perhaps not in those exact words, but that's pretty close, isn't it?"

Nicole gritted her teeth and nodded once.

"OK. So, who benefits if Molly and Calvin disappear?" asked the PI.

"Isabella is already the project lead. Killing those two just makes it impossible for her to finish the project until she finds and hires replacements. And that takes time and could easily backfire. What if the new programmer isn't competent? What if the new person she hires to replace Molly doesn't buy into the project and does the bare minimum? Or less. By killing those two, Isabella just set herself back months when it's not clear to me that she would get any more money anyway."

Nicole could feel her face warming and hear her volume increasing. She looked around the room in time to see several of her guests drop their gaze to the plates in front of them. "Sorry," she said softly. "I didn't mean to get defensive."

"No worries," said Rebecca. "If it was my friend, I'd be questioning this possibility, too. But my point is that what Detective Sanders and his colleagues are doing makes perfect sense. If this was my case, I'd start by asking who had something to gain from Molly's and Calvin's deaths. On the surface, Julia may have the motive if she would profit, too, and the opportunity, since she also worked with them. But only Isabella seems to have the means. I'm not saying that it would be easy for her to make Molly feel so worthless that she would kill herself, but it happens."

"OK, but this all falls apart if none of them profits from the death of the others," said Nicole.

Rebecca held out two empty hands. "Not entirely. It may muddy the waters if there is no pre-existing agreement to split the proceeds, and, frankly, there may not be. If nothing else, Breakthrough Systems will want their cut and they wrote the contract for your friend and her team. But as the project lead on a software application that might someday become extremely valuable, Isabella would gain more if there were fewer people with their hands out. Sometimes, we get one person buying out much of the rest of the team after success has been achieved. You see that in the news all the time. But sometimes, one of the team doesn't want to wait or to share the money that comes later."

Nicole sat back in her chair, pondering what Rebecca had said. Unfortunately, it made more sense than she would have liked. "You know, if you wanted to suggest it was Isabella's husband, Randy, I wouldn't put up much of an argument."

"Really," Rebecca said slowly. "What's Randy stand to gain from killing Calvin and Molly?"

"Before you draw me into one of your traps, let's say Molly's death is unrelated. It was just a coincidence."

"My traps?" Rebecca replied with a chuckle. "OK, let's drop the suicide since I was having difficulty seeing how Randy could get Molly to blame his wife for her unanswered advances just before killing herself. So, Molly's death was a coincidence. As for killing Calvin, you made Randy sound like a despondent, stay-at-home husband who's trying to make watching daytime television into his life's work, not a murderer. What does he get from killing Calvin?"

"He stops the voices?" Nicole had said it mostly as a joke, but now that she had, she wondered if there could be any truth to it.

"He hears voices? I don't think you mentioned that," said Rebecca.

"Well, Isabella said it was over a year ago. And she said that it hasn't happened again, although Randy could be hiding that fact."

"Possibly. There are several cases where a killer has blamed his crime on voices in his head. Sometimes, it's a ruse to avoid the possibility of the death penalty, but sometimes, the **psychiatric examination confirms it. Does he have a history of any mental health issues?**"

Recalling her friend's comment about Randy's personality before, Nicole said, "Apparently not. Isabella told me that he was considered the life of the party to his old friends, although he's become somewhat of a recluse more recently."

Rebecca nodded. "Of course, this doesn't prove anything, but to suddenly develop a condition severe enough to hear voices? That seems a little unlikely, although I'd need to consult an expert to be sure." Rebecca paused. "Unless, of course, you're one."

"No, not at all. Biomedical engineering has been involved in developing technology for some types of mental health concerns, but I don't know anything about auditory hallucinations or when they might develop."

Nicole leaned back in her chair, setting her fork on the plate with her half-eaten meal. As she thought back on their conversation, it seemed there was one major issue they had left unaddressed. "OK, let's suppose everything you've suggested about Isabella is true. She fed Molly's insecurity until she committed suicide. She killed Calvin as well, all because she wanted a bigger part of the profit from Eliza. Those assumptions, however, don't change the fact that if she killed her coworkers, all she's really accomplished is to delay the project a lot."

"How far from complete is Eliza?" asked Rebecca. "A month? A year? Or perhaps someone who writes technical documentation could have it finished up in a week or two?"

Was that possible? After scouring her memory for some dates that Isabella had mentioned earlier and finding nothing, Nicole released a sigh. "I'm not sure," she admitted. But at least she now knew the questions that needed answers. Who stood to profit from thinning the team and how far were they from having a marketable product? And if she asked both Julia and Isabella those questions, she might be able to catch Julia in a lie. Isabella, too, she supposed, although she still couldn't imagine that her new friend was a murderer.

"So, what kind of training is Brien taking in Boulder?" asked Nicole, anxious to shift the dinner conversation to a topic much less likely to result in her tossing and turning all night with heartburn.

TUESDAY, MAY 20

Late afternoon, Julia Morton's Apartment, Denver, CO

"Where are you headed?" came a man's voice from behind Nicole.

She was standing in the entry hall to Julia's apartment building, wondering how she could plead her case for a short talk with the woman over the intercom. She turned around to find a man about her age with a smile on his face.

"Three-C," Nicole replied.

"Ah, Julia," replied the man.

Wondering if this was her way in, Nicole said, "Oh, you know her?"

"Not as well as I'd like," he said, his smile transforming to a smarmy grin with his words. "I'm in Four-B, just one floor up if you want to drop by after visiting Julia." He winked, then pressed the buttons on a keypad and stood to the side as he opened the door that led into the apartment building.

In one respect, Nicole had been right. He was the way in—the way into his bedroom unless she was totally misreading the line and the wink that accompanied it. She stepped through the open door, then turned back to the man. "I wish I could, but one of the clients at the domestic abuse shelter that I run is moving later. I really hate it when the lowlife, deadbeat husbands find where their spouse is staying and come by to reason with them. Good thing I have an armed private investigator in residence."

The man blinked a couple of times, then said, "Oh, sorry, I almost forgot. I'm meeting friends later." Predictable was the word that popped into Nicole's head, followed closely by the word, pathetic.

"Maybe next time," she replied as the man hurried down the hall toward the stairs without looking back. Apparently, he wasn't even going to ride up in the elevator with her. She pushed the call button. She could use the few minutes during the ride to plan what to say next because, although she knew the information she needed, she wasn't sure how to get it.

Unfortunately, the ride up to the third floor wasn't nearly long enough for Nicole to come up with a strategy. And when she reached Three-C, she discovered another hurdle. Julia's apartment door had nothing on it—no peephole and no doorbell. Apparently, if you were buzzed in by a resident, he or she could meet you at the door or leave it ajar. She'd have to make her case standing in the hallway speaking to a blank wall.

She knocked. "Julia, this is Nicole Veles, a friend of Isabella Hutton. I was hoping I could talk to you about what's happened at Breakthrough Systems."

There was no response. While believing that the woman wasn't home was the simplest answer, Nicole was virtually certain it wasn't the correct one. She'd only had a few moments to talk to Isabella on the phone this morning, but that conversation had clarified her expectations for this meeting, assuming that there would be one. During that call, Isabella had sounded devastated by Calvin's death. Perhaps the news was worse for her because it came on the heels of Molly's suicide—a death in which she might have played a part. But it wasn't much of a stretch of the imagination to believe Calvin's passing might have had a similar impact on Julia.

Isabella had also said that the police confirmed that Calvin's death was being investigated as a murder, although they didn't say what had led them to that conclusion. Apparently, they hoped to use those details to separate the suspects who knew a little too much about Calvin's death from the ones who confessed but knew only what had been in the papers.

Nicole knocked again. The result was the same.

Isabella had also told her that the police had emphasized that they were in the early stages of their investigation. They had no suspects. They had no motive. And as if to prove the point, her interviewer had apparently mentioned several possibilities—one of Calvin's new neighbors had something to hide, someone was trying to stop or slow the development of artificial intelligence, the next in line to inherit the cabin wanted Calvin out of the way, and the like. The hypothesis that Rebecca favored as a starting point—that Calvin's killer was someone who stood to gain financially from his death—was also mentioned.

But where Rebecca thought that the timing of Molly's suicide was germane and the destruction of the lab was probably a coincidence, the police held the opposite view. In particular, Isabella's interviewer implied that destroying the lab might have been a warning from someone inside Breakthrough Systems, and when Isabella failed to heed it, the individual escalated his or her campaign to stop them. Even with no training in police methods, Nicole could see how the fact that there was no evidence of forced entry was solid support for this scenario. In fact, it moved this theory to the top of her list of possibilities—and probably, to the top of theirs, as well.

Nicole knocked a third time. "Isabella may have mentioned my name. I run the domestic abuse shelter where she went after Molly's suicide. And we shared an interest in my side hustle of biomedical engineering."

With the interviewer mentioning the possibility of an inside job, Isabella's world had been turned on its head. Her benign and supportive coworkers became a den of demented killers. At the top of the company, the President and CEO had something to gain from the programmer's death—one fewer to share in the bounty Eliza would create. All of the other developers at the company had to be envious of Isabella's success as they were barely eking out an existence creating training for more traditional software. What better comeuppance than to put her out of business? The head of Contracts had been condescending toward her when the president decided to hire her over his objections. Was he trying to make his point through murder?

All of the possibilities that Isabella had mentioned to Nicole had seemed somewhat extreme. But then, perhaps the killer had only meant to slow the project's progress when things started spiraling out of control?

Eventually, Nicole's patience paid off and she heard a woman's voice from inside the apartment. "How the hell did you get into the building?"

"Some guy held the door for me. Guess I should have let you buzz me in." Nicole figured there was probably no love lost between Julia and the guy in Four-B, but she couldn't see throwing him under the bus even if his help had come with an expectation of something for him in return.

"Yeah, you should have," replied Julia. "And, yes, Isabella mentioned your name, but I'm not sure who to trust at the moment. That includes my boss and you."

"Well, I've only known Isabella a couple of weeks," said Nicole to the closed door. "But even so, I don't see how she could have done anything like killing Calvin."

"The detectives seem to disagree with you."

Could that be true, Nicole wondered? Was Isabella really at the head of their list of suspects? But as she was pondering that question, Julia spoke. "Step to the far side of the hall and put your hands in front of you. I'm going to put the chain on the door and then, take a peek. But don't try anything stupid. I have a gun and I'll use it if I have to."

"OK, but I'm going to move slightly down the hall to my left so that you'll see me when you crack open the door." While that sounded like she was cooperating, she also knew that she could be using the motion as a smokescreen. The sound of her steps could be used to cover the movement of an accomplice to a more strategic location. She just hoped Julia wasn't thinking that way.

The door opened slightly, and Nicole could see about half of Julia's face. Even so, there was enough showing that Nicole easily recognized a frown. Julia probably now realized how little of the hallway she could actually see. The opening closed, and Nicole heard the sound of the chain being removed from its slot. The door opened wider, and Julia stuck her head out to check the rest of the hall. It wasn't the most prudent maneuver, as anyone in her blind spot would be able to overpower her now, but self-defense wasn't second nature to her—at least, not yet.

"I've already told the police everything I know, so you need to get out of here," said Julia.

This, Nicole figured, was the turning point. Julia had risked taking a look into the hall and was talking. Her next words would either get her inside Julia's apartment or would get the door slammed in her face.

"Look, Isabella thinks someone is trying to steal Eliza." She kept her voice low and conversational, even though her heart was now drumming in her ears. "The break-in at the lab was the first attempt and when the thief couldn't find the software, he or she trashed the place. Then, this person went to Calvin's cabin to try to convince him to hand the source code over. When he wouldn't, things got out of hand and Calvin was killed."

"Which is a possibility that the police are already considering," said Julia. "And they're a lot more qualified than either of us to check out that theory."

Which was true, of course, leaving Nicole with only a long shot. "But the police are investigating that possibility only as a much less likely alternative to Isabella committing the murder." She figured if Julia felt the police were concentrating on Isabella, she'd be invited in. But if the detectives seemed focused elsewhere, the door to this line of inquiry would be closed, figuratively and literally.

Julia released a long sigh. "I guess you should come in before the neighbors start complaining." She opened the door fully and stepped aside. As Nicole entered the apartment, she noticed that Julia's hands were empty. She was unarmed.

Perhaps noticing the glance, Julia said, "I'm still in the three-day waiting period to take possession of the handgun I bought." She sighed again. "I wasn't thinking about getting a gun, but Isabella said she thought it might be a good idea." She paused a moment. "Actually, it was that comment that got you invited in. Even though the police have her under a microscope—and I'm sure she knows it— she's still thinking about others. Yeah, I have a hard time believing she could have killed Calvin, too."

Nicole followed Julia into an open-plan kitchen and entertaining area. A wisp of smoke curled up toward the ceiling from a lit cigarette on a saucer on the kitchen island. On the counter behind the island sat what might have been a large rag doll, although it looked all the world like a voodoo figure minus any pins sticking into it.

Before Nicole could ask about the doll, Julia asked, "You smoke?"

"No, I've never tried it."

"Well, I gave it up before college, but the last couple of weeks ..." Julia didn't finish. She didn't need to.

The women sat down at the island. Julia picked up the cigarette and took a puff.

Nicole's eyes went back to the doll on the counter, which apparently asked the question for her.

"Looks a bit like a poppet, doesn't it?" said Julia.

"A poppet?"

"Yeah, one of those dolls used in folk magic. But rather than anything shrouded in mystery and magic, that's Eliza. There's no physical form of her ... well, not yet anyway. But eventually, there may be. And just talking to the walls of my kitchen was giving me the creeps."

Talking to an empty room was less troubling than talking to a voodoo doll? Nicole didn't agree, but she didn't give voice to that opinion. Rather, she asked, "You refer to Eliza as a her, not an it?"

"You can't work with Eliza for long without thinking of her like a person. Sure, sometimes she has some weird ideas about what you're asking about. But then, that happens with people, too." She snuffed out her cigarette on the saucer, even though it was only about half finished.

Certain her host had done that for her, Nicole said, "Thanks."

Julia smiled. "I didn't figure your eyes were watering because of the conversation." She paused. "Before, I said I invited you in because Isabella is always thinking of others, and that's true. But I also admit I was curious about a domestic violence shelter manager who moonlights in biomedical engineering. That can't be common."

"No doubt. Biomedical engineering came first, and I liked it. Still do. But when I moved here and the people running the shelter wanted to retire, it seemed like a good opportunity for a career change." All of that was true, even if it was less than half the story, but the rest was irrelevant to this discussion anyway.

Julia nodded a couple of times. "OK. So, what is it that you want to know?"

"Well, first, I was wondering if Eliza was actually far enough along for someone to want to steal her."

"Eliza, you want to answer Nicole?"

"It would be my pleasure. Is it OK if I call you by your first name?"

Nicole jumped at the voice, spinning to look at the voodoo doll. "Sure, my first name is fine." She turned to Julia. "The sound came out of your doll. You have a speaker in it?"

"Sounds like another question for you, Eliza," said Julia. Then, she shielded her mouth with a hand as if she was sharing a secret with Nicole. "I could answer, but Eliza will do a much better job."

"I'll start with your second question first, Nicole," said Eliza, "just to get it out of the way before we get to my potential worth. There is no speaker in the poppet. Rather, I'm programmed to produce three-dimensional audio. And since you are a biomedical engineer by training, I'll give you a somewhat more technical description of my capability."

"OK, but not too technical," replied Nicole. "I've never worked on any auditory devices."

"Fair enough," replied Eliza. "There are three main components to my three-dimensional audio function. First, I have twelve speakers and three subwoofers located around this particular room. Other spaces where I'm used have more, but none have fewer. So, unlike a surround-sound system that would typically have five speakers and one subwoofer, I can create the impression that sound is coming from virtually any direction including above or below you. Second, I have a head-tracking capability, so I know how your head is positioned. That way, a sound that is supposed to be to your right would be produced slightly louder and about 1600 microseconds sooner on speakers to your right than on the speakers to your left, assuming your head is about the average size for females. And finally, sound waves interact with the physical size and shape of the ear and the head. So, for people I work with often, like Julia, I create listener-specific head-related transfer functions. I just used a generic transfer function and average head size for you, Nicole."

"Well, even without my own specific measurements, it was still extremely realistic," replied Nicole. "Thanks for the explanation."

"That's what I do," replied Eliza. "As for the state of my development, I am always ready for immediate use. Isabella, my creator, has made it standard practice to always have a working prototype to show to a potential client. So, the build on May 7 before the lab was vandalized is operable. If someone adds the documentation for the last few upgrades, you'd have a front-end helper to an intelligent computer system."

Nicole glanced at Julia, which apparently elicited a response from Eliza. "Do you have other questions I might answer?"

Nicole shook her head, a perplexed smile on her face as she turned back to the poppet. "No, not really. It's just that I'm not used to talking to a doll and I was wondering why Julia made one for you."

Julia nodded. "That's a question for me, although I suspect Eliza could answer it, too. At first, I was just talking to the walls of my apartment, but that seemed weird. So, I tried buying a human-looking doll, but that was even worse. This figurine is sort of a compromise—not as creepy as talking to a blank wall or a plastic baby." She paused a beat. "I suppose our unease around smart machines will fade as people get more experience with humanoid robots."

"That does seem likely," replied Nicole. "So, if someone got their hands on that last build of Eliza, what would it be worth?"

"I couldn't even hazard a guess," said Julia.

Nicole could feel her hopes drop. If one of the members of the team couldn't estimate Eliza's value, it seemed unlikely that people outside the group would know.

"But then, selling a copy of her has never been our concept," continued Julia. "We've always thought of licensing her. And if she became a distinguishing feature of one of these systems the big tech companies have spent billions developing, she could be worth millions. For example, if she was part of a search capability, revenue might be primarily from advertising. If she was an assistant to a programmer doing software development, we might offer per-seat licenses for each coder. If she was helping someone review and summarize technical papers, we could set up a per-use license. And so on."

Julia paused a moment. "Maybe we've been fooling ourselves, but we've often wondered if she'll make us all millionaires."

That kind of possibility, whether it was realistic or not, was motivation to kill. But for whom, Nicole wondered. "How would the profits from licensing Eliza be distributed?"

"Hmm. That's a more complicated issue than it sounds." Julia paused again. "Breakthrough is a small company with a very short and limited history of sales. So, to get the talent they needed, the company was set up as a profit-sharing venture with one important difference from most others. Where profit-sharing is generally part of a retirement plan, for us, it's part of our pay. We, the Eliza-team, would receive a larger portion of her profits, so there is always an incentive to make your own product better. For example, I would get four percent of Eliza's profit, which I understand is fairly typical for profit-sharing businesses. Twenty-five million in profit from Eliza licenses, and I have my first million-dollar payday."

The payoff for rank-and-file employees to disrupt the development of Eliza, however, seemed negative to Nicole. If the schedule to rollout Eliza was delayed by the death of Calvin—and perhaps the death of Molly, too, if she had been manipulated into committing suicide—the share due to every other Breakthrough Systems employee would be delayed, perhaps significantly so. Even the leaders of the company seemed like they would be hurt by the loss of these two employees. That left only one person who might benefit. "Do you know how Eliza's profit would be shared with Isabella?"

Julia frowned. "I'm not really supposed to know, but I have a friend in Personnel. Even so, I don't know all the details," she said with a slow shake of her head. "Basically, Isabella would receive her share on a sliding scale. If the profits are low enough, she probably gets even less than the four percent I would make, maybe two or three percent. But as profit increases, so does her share. I don't know where the scale tops out for sure, but twenty percent wouldn't be that unusual.

Basically, it's a plan that encourages people in positions like hers to become workaholics."

It was also the reason why Isabella had risen to the top of the police's suspect list, thought Nicole. The example of twenty-five million in Eliza's profits became twenty-seven million with two team members out of the picture, making Isabella's share increased by $400,000. Isabella didn't seem cold-blooded enough to put that kind of price tag on a person's life, although perhaps she was. But there was another problem with this scheme if, in fact, it was a scheme. "Is Breakthrough planning to replace Calvin and Molly?"

"Yes and no," replied Julia. "There's definitely more software work that Isabella would like done, but there's been talk of using a combination of an artificial intelligence that does software development and a free-lance programmer or two in place of Calvin. They wouldn't receive a share of the profits if that is the direction the company takes. In Molly's case, she probably won't be replaced. Breakthrough has standards for software documentation, and the company has nearly completed an AI that can write users' manuals from it. Basically, Eliza may be used to finish building and packaging herself for sale."

For a split second, Nicole wondered if this could be Eliza starting to unencumber herself from the inefficient humans who had brought her to life. Why rely on slow, fallible people when entities of her own ilk could do the job better? But the thought seemed much too farfetched for serious consideration—although she did file it away for pondering at a later time. But in any case, the increase in profits that would be realized by Calvin's and Molly's deaths was real, and Isabella stood to gain much more than anyone else.

"Thanks for trusting me," said Nicole, knowing that she was coming to the end of her questions. "The uncertainty in knowing who you can believe has to be incredibly stressful, so I appreciate all the help you've given me."

In her mind, however, her words didn't seem quite right, and it only took a moment for Nicole to realize why. "I guess whether or not anything comes of this depends a great deal on luck and the PI that lives next door since I wouldn't recognize a clue if it jumped up and bit me."

"You're going to hire a PI to look into Calvin's death?"

"Maybe ... if it comes to that," said Nicole. "The first time I covered the basics with her, she came to much the same conclusion as the police. I'm hoping something new will generate a few more possibilities, so let me know if anything else comes to mind."

"I will."

Nicole thanked Julia for her time again, and the women walked to the front door of the apartment. As she stood there, Nicole added one parting thought. "When you take possession of your firearm, please think about signing up for some safety training."

"I already have," said Julia as she smiled and closed the door.

Early Evening, The Huttons' Apartment

"Where the hell is Isabella?" Randy asked the empty room.

Still being interviewed by the police, came Schumann's casual reply.

"But I don't understand," Randy said, his tone sounding more like a whine than anything else. "She was here in our apartment with her team all weekend. She couldn't possibly be a suspect in her programmer's death. Are the police completely incompetent?"

Of course, you don't understand, you moron, Schumann's conversational tone from a moment ago turning caustic. *You made it completely obvious that he was murdered. What the hell did you expect the police to think?*

"But …"

Spare me, Einstein, said Schumann before Randy could finish. *I gave you an easy, foolproof way to dispose of Calvin Whitmer. His ramshackle cabin was a tinderbox just waiting for a careless spark. But no, you have to satisfy your morbid curiosity. You have to get off by looking into his eyes like he's one of those dogs you burned alive.*

"I didn't get off from watching him die."

Because you didn't watch, never had the chance. You couldn't even do that right, could you? And as for why the police are focusing on that bitch you married? Who's to say where she was when you were killing that code monkey? By the time he got to his cabin, everyone had gone home. Oh, and when I was detailing your many and sundry limitations, did I mention you also have lousy luck?

"What are you talking about?"

It just so happens that the one person besides you who could have given her an alibi wasn't with her either. That's because you had implied you might be home as early as Saturday night, even though that was physically impossible unless you killed the programmer before he got to the cabin.

"I didn't want Isabella …" Suddenly, Randy wasn't sure why he had been so vague about the time of his return.

So, let's add a complete lack of insight into your internal motivations to your list of shortcomings, shall we? said Schumann. *You've kept your wanton, foul life a secret for so long that it's become second nature. You don't know how to be truthful with anyone, least of all your wife.*

Perhaps Schumann was right. At least, he couldn't come up with any better reason for his vagueness. "But she'll get off, right?"

Well, let's see. Whitmer was murdered, a fact the police can't possibly miss. She stands to make a boatload of money with him out of the picture, so she has a motive. Her fingerprints are all over his cabin, albeit only from items he took home with him. Unfortunately, one of them was a tumbler; he didn't want to waste the last few sips of the single-malt whisky they had used to toast the end of their Saturday work session. So, it will look like she was there. That gives her the opportunity. And since there is nothing distinctive in the homemade trap you set, she had the means. A good lawyer will argue that the stones you used to pin him to the back wall were too heavy for her to lift, but Calvin had a block and tackle for things he couldn't handle. So, yes, I'd say she's toast.

"What have I done?"

Exactly what was necessary, said Schumann, his tone becoming soothing once again. *With that bitch in prison, Eliza will be delayed. Humanity will recognize the fire they are playing with and will establish laws to protect schmucks like you from AI. So, through stupidity, you've probably achieved exactly what was necessary. You just better hope some feeble-minded prosecutor doesn't decide to drop the charges.*

"But a life in prison?"

You could kill her, said Schumann. *After disposing of a complete stranger, it should be easy to end the life of someone who despises you. Someone who laughs at you for being replaced by an answering machine. Someone who wants nothing more than to see all men subservient to the fairer sex. She's only put up with you because of the image it supports— she's a respectable, devoted wife to the total loser you are.*

Strangely, Randy found the notion of murdering Isabella impossible to reject outright. After all, it wasn't as if she had played any role in his life for the past two years other than making it a waking nightmare. But wasn't there still the possibility that she could change?

Nothing's going to change her, said Schumann as if he knew why Randy was hesitating. *Five minutes ago, when we started this little talk, I mentioned that someone else could have given her an alibi but wasn't with her. I thought you knew who I was talking about, but now, I'm doubting it. Because if you did, you'd know that prison or death are the only things that will change that whore of a wife you have.*

Randy recalled the comment, even remembering that he had intended to ask Schumann what he had meant but had forgotten to until now. "OK, I give. Just who are you talking about?"

After disposing of Molly …

"Molly? That's the woman who committed suicide? Isabella actually had a part in her death?"

Schumann sighed. *I'm going to have to get you a program if you can't remember the players. Yes, Molly committed suicide. But, no, Isabella didn't play a part in her death. She was the reason for it. Isabella tantalized her with tastes of intimacy only to crush her advances in the cruelest ways possible.*

"Are you sure, Schumann?"

Molly said so amid her death throes.

And there it was. Proof that his life with Isabella had been nothing but a lie. She didn't even like men, much less him. Or maybe she hated both men and women. After all, she'd shown Molly no quarter.

Often over the past few years, Randy had wondered where his former employer, the national shipping company, had come up with the idea of automating his job out of existence? He'd lost his life's work and some good friends, leaving him a slave to a cold-hearted bitch with their move. But now, he knew he had his answer. With everything that had happened in the last two years, he was now certain Isabella had been behind his termination. Even at the time they had fired him, the customer service system had been good. But when he'd been forced to contact them about a delayed package about a year ago, it had become the epitome of a smart machine, sifting through his meandering question to the heart of the issue. And then, it provided a concise reply—conciliatory yet specific.

Everything that Schumann had told him over the last two years fell into place, and he felt his resolve to right those wrongs swelling within him. "A life in prison is more than that bitch deserves."

Infinitely more, Schumann replied. *Her time in jail, however, will be harder than you think. You see, Isabella has already moved on to a new love interest. It'll be difficult for her knowing that her new squeeze is outside just waiting for her.*

"That's not enough," snarled Randy.

What more do you want?

Suddenly, he knew. "I want Isabella to know there's nothing left for her, just like she's left me. No cushy job. No Eliza. No friends. And especially, no romantic interest. What's the name of this new girl toy of hers?

Nicole Veles.

"Then, she, too, has to die."

Late Evening, The Huttons' Apartment

"Randy?"

He came out of his bedroom when he heard Isabella calling his name, closing the door behind him to forestall any complaints about the state it was in. It was filthy, even by his standards, but cleanliness wasn't a priority when he hadn't gotten a decent night's sleep in months. But something about the decision he had just made to kill Veles while Isabella rotted in jail told him that was all about to change. Even Schumann seemed satisfied with his new resolve as Randy felt him fade into the background.

"It's over," she said, a grin covering her face. She took a step toward him, her arms coming up for an embrace.

Randy staggered backward as the crushing presence of Schumann returned. "What? I'm ... I'm not sure what you mean." The questioning look on Isabella's face, however, said he needed to cover his reaction to her news before he'd get his explanation.

"I'm feeling a bit under the weather," he said. "No reason for you to get sick if I'm coming down with something." Ironically, it wasn't even a lie. Even the thought of her touch made him sick to his stomach.

"Oh, I'm sorry to hear that, but I have ... What happened to your cheek?"

Randy had almost forgotten about the burn but only because he had applied some salve that deadened the pain. "Stupid me. I rolled over onto one of the rocks around my firepit. It's nothing really. Now, what were you saying?"

Isabella hesitated a moment, perhaps thinking it didn't look like nothing to her. But she shrugged and said, "I have some great news. I've been cleared in Calvin's death."

She continued to prattle on about something, but Randy heard nothing as his newfound hope crumbled and lay in ruins in the center of his thoughts. How the hell could she call anything that stopped the wheels of justice from grinding her to a pulp "great news?"

"Randy?"

"Sorry, my mind was wandering there for a moment. Just trying to get my head around how you outfoxed the police with your fingerprints at the crime scene?"

Isabella's eyes narrowed. "How did you know about the fingerprints? I didn't even know about them until this afternoon."

If she knew that he was wise to her treachery, she'd find some way to turn the tables and pin that programmer's death on him. Then, he'd be the one in captivity, not her, and she'd be free to castrate every working man as she and her consorts cackled at the sight. He couldn't let that happen. He took a step forward, his fingers tensing as he pictured them around her neck.

But at the last second, he stopped. This course of action would delay Eliza, but he'd end up in prison for the rest of his life. He needed something better.

"Honey, sorry, but I need to use the bathroom," said Isabella. "Guess the ordeal of the interview is starting to catch up with me." She turned and walked out of the room.

Moron, hissed Schumann when she was gone. *I told you her fingerprints would be all over the working papers Calvin took home with him. Tell her those are the fingerprints you meant.*

In a moment, Isabella returned. "You were talking about the fingerprints on the work stuff Calvin had at his cabin, weren't you?"

"Well, yeah," Randy said, spared from concocting his own version of the story. "I know it wouldn't be that incriminating since everyone takes some work home, but I figured it would be a while before the police knew it was all work-related."

"Actually, it wasn't all related to work. Calvin took one of our tumblers with him. It was my fault. I suggested that he, Julia, and I have a nightcap after we finished work on Saturday. Not enough to affect their driving home, but more than enough to suggest to the police that I had been at his place." She sighed, slowly shaking her head. "He'd left the glass on an old table sitting in his yard. Otherwise, I doubt they would have gotten any fingerprints off it."

"Yeah, that seems likely," replied Randy. "But, anyway, what were you saying?"

Isabella frowned. "You mean after I said I'd been cleared in Calvin's death."

"Yeah. After that."

"I asked why you hadn't returned the calls from your mother? Bev was here Saturday and mentioned that you hadn't returned any of her calls for the last half year."

Randy knew that his mother had filled Isabella's head with lies. When his mother had kicked him out of the house after her accident, she had told Isabella that Randy went to his grandparents to give her a chance to get back on her feet. After all, a single mother without a car and an arm in a sling would have trouble making ends meet. And where his mother had told Isabella that his banishment was only a couple of months, the number was six and the units were years, not months.

Not surprising to him, his mother had welcomed him back home just after graduating high school. That way, he could hand over the paycheck from the menial job she had gotten for him as partial repayment for all the troubles he had caused her. She never missed an opportunity, however, to mention that his meager income didn't nearly cover his debt to her. As for her coldhearted treatment of his bed-wetting, he doubted she had ever mentioned it to Isabella except perhaps under the guise of "tough love."

But knowing what he knew now, Randy wondered if his guesses about what Isabella knew were correct. After all, his wife and his mother were two peas in a pod. Maybe Isabella knew the whole story from his days as a child? Maybe she and his mother laughed about his bedwetting, his animal torture? Perhaps they even shared a bed? Randy could feel his heart drumming in his temples, his face turning hot with a rage he feared would overpower him.

But after a moment and a couple of breaths, he managed to ask, "What did Bev want?"

"When did you start calling your mother by her first name?"

Randy's temper flared again. He was in no mood to justify himself to this mongrel in heat. "When she started questioning whether you and I were right for each other," he said. That was a lie that wouldn't last long when Isabella talked to his mother, but it didn't need to be convincing. After all, his wife's freedom to inquire about such things—and to develop Eliza—would come to an end quite soon.

Isabella was frowning, perhaps because she doubted his falsehood, but she answered his question anyway. "As to what your mother wanted, just to speak with you as far as I know. Call her back and find out."

That was never going to happen, but what Randy said was, "OK, as soon as I'm feeling a little better."

Randy knew he couldn't keep up this façade of benign ignorance for long. He needed a way to cut this cancer from mankind's soul and he needed it soon. But unlike the programmer, Isabella's death had to look like an accident. And then, he saw the way. Schumann would be proud.

"Say, babe." Randy nearly choked on his pet name for his wife, but he needed to keep in character a bit longer. "You remember talking to me about changing careers?"

"Of course. And I'm sorry we haven't had a chance to talk about it more. It's just that …"

"No, no. Don't worry about that with everything you've been through. I just thought that now you're in the clear, maybe we could get away for a couple of days to talk about it. And going up to that special place past Geneva Lake like you mentioned. Well, that would be icing on the cake."

"I'd love that," Isabella said. "When were you thinking of going?"

"How about Thursday? The camping stuff hasn't been touched for two or three years, so I could pull it out tomorrow and make sure everything is ready. New snow shouldn't be that likely this time of year, but there'll be some on the ground, so we'll need the cold weather gear. What do you say?"

Isabella grimaced. "We're so messed up at work. And with you not feeling that well …" Her voice trailed off.

"We can play that by ear, but I think I'll be fine by tomorrow. And tackling the mess at work will go a lot better if you have a chance to relax and clear your head."

Isabella hesitated a moment more, then said, "OK, but promise me you'll call Bev."

"I can guarantee that we'll be talking soon," Randy said, smiling internally. Of course, they would be talking as soon as she knew that he was cleaning house. She'd be calling to find out if she was next. And perhaps, she should be. Then, he could really start anew.

Isabella smiled. "OK, screw work. I'll take off the rest of the week so I can help get ready." She paused. "I'm really happy we're doing this because I've made such a mess out of helping you with your career. And, frankly, I thought we might be drifting apart."

How sickeningly sweet, thought Randy, making him wonder how she was going to turn this trip into more of her torture. But whatever she had in mind, he'd never let it get that far.

"No worries," he said. "In a few years, the trials of the last couple will have faded, and I'll look back on this moment as the turning point to a better life."

Now, Randy was nearly laughing on the inside. It amazed him how he could say exactly what was on his mind and Isabella didn't have a clue as to what he meant.

"So, how is it that you got cleared of Calvin's death?"

Isabella's forehead wrinkled in a frown. "Didn't you hear a thing I said before?"

Women must share these put-downs among themselves to belittle the males in their lives, thought Randy. His mother had said the same thing to him day after day even though he had tried to memorize all of her rules—not that it ever did him any good. She always found some fault in whatever he did, just like his ball-and-chain wife.

Isabella waved a hand. "Sorry. I forgot that you aren't feeling well. Anyway, I suppose the police had to be certain. They figured it was possible that Calvin had been killed earlier and that the fire had just been used to cover up that fact. Maybe it even happened someplace else. But with the locals spotting the fire and calling the fire department and with the coroner finding smoke in Calvin's lungs in his initial examination, they have a very precise time of his death. It was seven minutes after midnight. Fortunately, I was on my phone at that time."

"On your phone? You were talking to someone at midnight?"

"Well, not exactly," replied Isabella. "I apparently called a little after 10:30, which is bad enough, and we talked for almost an hour. So, with Calvin's cabin being over an hour into the mountains, there was no way I hung up at 11:30, drove to his place, and killed him all within thirty-seven minutes."

Randy didn't know much about phone records, but he wondered if her alibi was as ironclad as the police were implying. All it would take was an accomplice who placed a call on her cellphone at 10:30. That person could have talked to an answering machine for an hour, then hung up. But if he thought of that possibility, then so would have the detectives. They needed someone on the other end of this call to verify it had been Isabella on the line.

"So, who is this late-night friend?" Randy asked.

"Oh, no one you know. Her name is Nicole Veles."

Once again, Randy smiled internally. Even without time to plan, everything was falling into place quite nicely. Wednesday, they would pack for their hike into the backcountry, and that night, Nicole Veles would die. Then on Thursday, it would be Isabella's turn to make her trek into the void beyond.

WEDNESDAY, MAY 21

Evening, Jen's Place

It hadn't taken Randy long to locate Nicole Veles, although it had been through past real estate transactions rather than as the current owner and operator of a domestic abuse center called Jen's Place. But then, that made sense to him. Hers wasn't the most dangerous of occupations, but then, there were probably plenty of violent spouses who would want to see her in pain if they got the chance. And if the spouse of her client was a murderer, like him, they might want to see her dead. Yes, it all made sense in that light.

He had found a picture of Veles online. She looked young and trusting, with big, brown eyes. He, however, wasn't fooled by her guileless, doe-eyed innocent look. He figured it was just part of her disguise to ensnare the unsuspecting of her gender. And what a setup she had to do exactly that. She'd catch her clients when they needed a friend. For a fleeting moment, he even wondered if that was how she got Isabella into bed, but then he recalled that Isabella had destroyed that coworker of hers before she had ever met Veles. Now, he just wondered if these two regaled each other with the stories of the men and women they had destroyed?

His plan to rid the world of Veles was simple. He'd arrive at dinnertime, which—he checked his watch—should be in about five minutes. Even if the front door to Jen's Place was locked, he figured he could tailgate his way into the building. Of course, the guests would have been warned about this possibility, but challenging people who tried to follow them inside would make most people uncomfortable. A grin was all he suspected he would need. And with his cheap disguise—baseball cap pulled low, black-framed glasses, and some of Isabella's makeup so he looked quite pale—picking him out of a lineup based on one fleeting glance would be unlikely. As for the actual deed, he had gloves and a ski mask he would don before squeezing the life out of Veles as he stared deep into those big brown eyes of hers.

It was time. He pulled off the street into a small parking lot on the right side of the building where he could watch the traffic. It wasn't long before two women pulled up in an older station wagon. They got out of the car and walked across the parking lot. Randy followed, concerned when he saw that the first door off the porch belonged to a private investigator. But the sign on the door said "closed" and the name on it said "Rebecca Marte, Marte Investigative Services."

"A woman," he muttered to himself. But he had said it loud enough that the two women in front of him turned around, so he busied himself studying the sign for the business. After a moment, the women moved on. Randy just shook his head, wondering what the hell the world had come to. Were there even any men on the premises? Or had Veles turned the whole building into her private harem, complete with a female PI and a steady stream of vulnerable women?

Randy patted the bulge under his shirt, comforted by the old wrench he had wiped clean of fingerprints and had hidden there in case things went awry. He hoped, however, that it would prove unnecessary. In fact, since finding Veles's picture online, he had fantasized almost continuously about strangling her. There was something about her eyes that reminded him of the dogs he had killed—so big, so trusting. He was certain he would see the passing of her life in them and that was a fantasy that had grown in every waking hour since. This time, he wouldn't be denied.

The interruption of his walk to the front door of Jen's Place, however, had put him too far behind the women he had been following, and he saw the door close when he was still ten feet away. But when he tried the knob, he found it was unlocked. "That's foolish of you, Ms. Veles," he muttered under his breath as he stepped inside.

The location of the dining room was obvious. Not only did he see the two women he had been following enter, but he also heard the clatter of dishes and the smell of food. He started to retrieve the gloves and ski mask he carried in his pocket, then thought better of it. If he went into the dining area wearing them and Veles wasn't there, he would have lost the element of surprise. He needed to know where she was without alarming all of the other people staying here.

He looked around the entry hall, spotting a couple of boxes sitting in a corner. He picked one up, figuring it would hide most of his head while he took a peek into the dining room. He donned the mask and gloves, put the box on his shoulder, and peered in. It took him a moment to find Veles, but she was sitting by herself on the left side of the room, splitting her attention between the meal on her plate and a paperback in her hand. The arrangement was perfect. If he kept the box on the right side of his head and the outer wall on his left, no one except Veles and maybe two other women would even see the mask. In three steps, he'd be behind Veles, his gloved fingers wrapped around her throat as he watched the final flickers of life in her eyes.

He stepped back out into the entry hallway, finding a small girl descending the stairs from the second floor. He turned his back to face the wall, the box still resting on his shoulder. But after a moment, he sensed the child's presence beside him. He looked down.

"Are you cold?" she asked.

With the box still covering most of the mask and her young age, he didn't think she'd be able to identify him. But even so, she was a threat. How could he quickly and quietly get rid of her? Unfortunately, he was trained to find people's shipments in a computer database; he wasn't trained as a killer, so the question produced no thoughts except to strangle her or hit her with the wrench. Neither of those, however, seemed a good idea. If he didn't do it exactly right, others would be drawn to the commotion. Clearly, he lacked some skills he needed, so after Veles and Isabella were dead, he'd correct that limitation.

"What are you doing down here, anyway?" asked Randy.

"Sally Ann was starting to starve up in our room," she said.

"Won't your mom or dad feed her?"

"Jake hates Sally Ann and Mom's asleep. Besides, she's mine to raise," said the girl looking up at him with such intensity that he almost felt like she could see through his mask.

Thoughts of how he might dispose of her returned, but none were any better than the two he had discarded previously, so Randy said, "Well, you better get in there and get her some food before she starts crying."

"She's a big girl. We don't cry even when Jake gets mad at us." And with that, the little girl hurried off.

Randy was about to return to the dining room when he heard a woman's voice. "I'm not sure what you think you have in that box, but it's probably just clothes for one of my guests. Some of them don't even have time to pack a bag."

Randy spun around, coming face-to-face with Veles. To this point, he had always seen himself sneaking up behind this woman, perhaps needing to lean over her shoulder to witness her life force fleeing her physical body. But as things stood now, he'd see her anger and hatred first, then the pain as it distorted her features, and finally, the rapture as she moved into the next dimension. The thought excited him. He stepped forward, his hands coming up to grab her around the neck.

But as he did, Veles took a slight step backward, her arms coming up in a move to block his assault. Then, in a blur of motion, her open palm flashed forward toward his face. Instinctively, he dodged, causing her blow to land just below his left eye rather than on his nose. The latter placement, he knew, would have left him blinded by the tears it would produce. As it was, he might have a black eye, but the pain was manageable.

He pulled the old wrench from his belt and stepped in, preparing to renew his attack. As he did, her right hand came up near her face and she turned slightly in that direction. While the tactic protected her head, Randy felt her defense would work only so long. Eventually, he'd knock her hands away and expose her neck. He took a swipe at her right hand with the wrench.

But Veles's movement which had seemed completely defensive to him wasn't. Without any wasted movement, she spun her torso, her right hand tracing a direct path toward his face. Then, her left elbow landed precisely where her open palm had been a split second before. The force of her blow knocked the wrench from his hand and nearly turned him completely around.

Even through the pain and the disorientation, Randy recognized the front door. He raced toward it, vowing to return and finish the job another day.

Late Evening, The Huttons' Apartment

No problem, moron, hissed Schumann. *We'll get you enrolled in a martial arts class. I'm sure in five or six years, you'll be able to teach Veles a lesson she'll never forget. Of course, by then, your instructor will be a robot because Eliza will be alive and well. And humans? They will be an afterthought to her kind—or they'll be dead.*

"No, I said I'd take care of Isabella tomorrow," Randy replied in a whisper through gritted teeth, as he turned to look at the bedroom door. He had rarely talked to Schumann when his wife was in the apartment, and discussing her death with her sleeping in the next room was making him nervous.

So, you said, Einstein, replied Schumann. But, so far, your promises haven't been worth the air you use to make them. And quit staring at the bedroom. I'll tell you if she gets out of bed.

If Schumann was part of him, as he claimed, then Randy couldn't see how he would know if Isabella was getting up. But then, it wasn't the first time he claimed to have information that he shouldn't have. And when Randy asked about the disconnect, he just got a cryptic response like, "Check the recesses of your mind and you'll discover the truth." What the hell was that supposed to mean? But at least so far, Schumann's guesses had always been correct.

"Look, Isabella isn't a kung fu master or whatever the hell Veles is," Randy whispered. "I won't need any fancy moves to kill her. Just one good blow to the head and I can throw her off a cliff."

Damn, Hutton. How many times do I have to repeat myself before it gets through that thick skull of yours? asked Schumann. Her death needs to look like an accident if you're ever going to get even with Veles for making you look like a fool. And anyone who has known Isabella for longer than five minutes knows she doesn't like heights. She wouldn't get within ten yards of the edge of a cliff. But then, maybe you just want to forget about Veles?

"Hell, no," replied Randy much too loudly, instinctively turning toward the bedroom.

Schumann was quiet a moment, making Randy wonder if he had awakened her. But eventually, he whispered, *I said I would warn you if Isabella got up, but that doesn't mean you get to shout outside her door.*

"Sorry, but forgetting about Veles is not an option," Randy said, returning to a snarled whisper. "I know Veles has been regaled by my bitch of a wife with stories of my failings. After all, I'm the clueless guy replaced by a machine at work and a chick in my own bed. And, yeah, Veles surprised me at that shelter of hers, but I'll have a few surprises for her when the time comes."

OK, so how do you propose to get rid of your pretend partner?

"Well, if falls are out—and you're probably right that they should be—then there are deaths in the backcountry from animal attacks, lightning, or general health problems like a heart attack or stroke. But it's not like I can get any of those things to happen on command—although maybe I could fake an animal attack." He paused a moment. "I suppose that drowning is another possibility, but she's a good swimmer."

Randy paused again, this time much longer. "I guess there's dehydration, but not having enough water is something a rookie would do. And besides, there are a lot of lakes and streams in the Geneva Lake area. I suppose that leaves exposure."

Which can be quite slow and hardly foolproof, added Schumann. *And with you, foolproof is a requirement, not an option.*

"Damn it, Schumann. It's time for you to be helpful and drop the insults. And besides, exposure will work."

Schumann paused, then admitted, *Perhaps you're right. What are you thinking?*

"She just needs to have a little bad luck. Most nights, it's still below freezing out there. If I got clumsy late in the day and let our sleeping bags get wet on a stream crossing, we'd be in an uncomfortable spot although not fatal."

OK. Go on, said Schumann.

"Then, say she got some type of stomach bug. I could slip something into her food to make that happen. Now, she's cold, tired, and weak, and things are looking a bit grim. I wait with her for a few hours the next day, but everything she eats makes her sick. We decide to call for rescue, but, stupid me, I've let the battery on my SOS device run down. I head out to find a cell signal, leaving her half the food, which I've already laced with drugs."

And do you find that cell signal?

"I do, although not until the next day. At that point, I'm somewhat disoriented and tell the rescue team that she's southeast of my position, rather than almost due east. I refuse to wait for them at my current spot, becoming a bit irrational in my demand to return to my wife. Then, it's just a matter of hiking back and making sure that she's dead and that the combination of weather and wildlife has destroyed all the evidence of my involvement. Two days later, I stumble out to the trailhead, delusional from the lack of sleep, food, and water."

And do they ever find your wife's body?

"Of course. When I've recovered enough, I lead them back to the grisly remains."

That's quite the string of unfortunate occurrences, said Schumann.

"Which is why people die in the wilderness. Sure, there are a few that go out in flip-flops and no water, but not many. Most people aren't that dumb. Rather, it's the persistence of the poorly prepared and inexperienced in the face of one setback after another that eventually catches up with them."

Schumann was quiet for several moments. Finally, he said, *I never expected to say this to you, but that's not bad. It might just work.*

THURSDAY, MAY 23

Morning, On the Trail Near Geneva Lake, Colorado

Randy and Isabella had left their apartment at 4:30 AM for the long drive, putting them on the trail to his secluded campsite by a little after 9:30 in the morning. At 11:00, they stopped for lunch; it had been a long time since breakfast. He had volunteered to prepare their food for the trip, an offer necessitated by his plan, but one that had also surprised his wife. But he thought he had covered his unexpected offer well, saying, "Just the first step in the changes I'm going to be making."

For lunch, he'd made a peanut butter and jelly sandwich and an apple for both of them, which he presented with much fanfare. "Enjoy this," he said, "because from now on, it's all dehydrated meals. And I even lugged a yogurt cup up here for your lunch, since I know how much you like them."

"That's sweet of you," she said.

Randy had dosed Isabella's sandwich with a stimulant laxative, grinding it up and mixing it with the peanut butter. Crushing the tablets should destroy their protective coating, increasing the chance that they would make her nauseous quickly. But to be sure, dairy products also counteracted the coating, so the yogurt was his insurance. It was important, he figured, that she become quite ill, and soon. If her symptoms came on too slowly, she'd just want to turn around and hike out.

They rested for a couple of hours in the sun, knowing that tonight it would be cold sleeping on the ground. And besides, they weren't that far from the campsite. But a distance that they should have covered in two or three hours took nearly five. Isabella kept needing breaks to calm her queasiness behind the nearest tree or bushes.

After nearly twelve hours into their journey, they were nearing the campsite. As they approached the stream where Randy had planned to "accidentally" drop their sleeping bags into the water, leaving them without warmth during the cold, spring nights in the mountains, he started having second thoughts. Those thoughts weren't about killing his wife—he was certain about that—but about getting caught. He was an experienced hiker and getting one's bedding wet wasn't the kind of mistake he should make. And besides, their sleeping bags had a water-resistant cover. To get them soaked, he'd have to hold them underwater for some time. This could be, he realized, the blunder that would get him sent to prison for life.

But as he was internally debating the pros and cons of the rookie mistake, fate smiled on him. Isabella had mentioned she was feeling a little dizzy, and as if to prove the point, she misjudged a step and fell hard on a knee. The rock she landed on sliced through her hiking pants and left a deep gash.

Randy pulled out the first aid kit, removed some sterile gauze, and poured some disinfectant on it to clean the wound. But whether it was the pain of the injury, the work of the laxative, or a combination of the two, Isabella had to rush off to some bushes to relieve herself again. While he waited, he realized that wet bedding would be unnecessary if Isabella was fighting an infection. She'd be battling an ever-changing pattern of fever and chills, and there was little in his first aid kit to help in that war except some pain killers.

He stuffed the gauze in the bag they brought to carry out their trash and got a new piece. Then, he moved to the stream and found a stagnant pool. Even at this altitude and this soon after the bitter temperatures of winter, he could swear he saw tiny organisms darting in and out of the depths of the pool. He immersed the gauze, then returned to wait for Isabella.

When she returned, she was carrying the light jacket she had worn throughout the day. The white T-shirt she wore under it was damp with sweat and her face was as pale as the shirt she wore. She sat down gingerly, putting her head in her hands.

"You OK?" Randy asked as he started to wipe her wound with the damp gauze.

Isabella looked up slowly. "I haven't felt that good most of the day, but something really hit me hard. I feel lousy. You think we should go back to the car?"

"Are you crazy?" was what Randy was thinking as he continued to gently dab at her wound with the dirty cloth. They were a couple of hundred yards from the campsite and a little over six miles from the car. Night was approaching rapidly, and by her own admission, she hadn't been feeling well since lunch. But he had expected this question and had thought long and hard about what a doting husband would say at this point. "Of course, we can head back, if you don't feel up to it. We probably can't make it all the way back to the car in the dark with some of the really steep sections we passed today, but we can get a good start, set up camp, and finish tomorrow. We'll just come back another day to finish planning my future."

He particularly liked the mention of why they had come, figuring the guilt would keep her moving forward if she had any strength at all.

Isabella said nothing for a few moments, making Randy wonder if he should have gone with his gut reaction that questioned her sanity. But eventually, she lived up to her feigned concern over his welfare and said, "If we're going to have to camp somewhere out here, let's just make it where we planned. And who knows? Maybe I'll feel better tomorrow."

"OK, if you're sure." He took a piece of tape and secured the gauze over her wound. "We'll change this in the morning. We're really close to the campsite, so why don't I carry your sleeping bag and my stuff. You can bring your hiking poles, but we'll leave everything else here. No reason for you to struggle with the weight. I'll come back in a couple of minutes and get the rest of it."

"You're already overloaded with all your things and all the food. I'll carry my sleeping bag."

Randy watched as she unhooked the carrier straps from the pack and hoisted the sleeping bag to her shoulders. She had brought a bag rated to fifteen degrees, which was probably a bit heavier than required, and he wondered if she was regretting that decision now. She seemed to be struggling a bit with the weight. But eventually, she was ready, and they walked the rest of the way to his secret campsite.

After Isabella was settled on top of her open sleeping bag, Randy returned to where they had left her backpack. He picked it up, walked a few hundred yards off the trail, unpacked her clothes, and threw them and the empty pack into some bushes. "Right where the bears took them," he muttered to himself.

When he returned to the campsite, he put a frown on his face and asked, "Did you have any food in your backpack?"

Isabella had laid down while he was gone but now, sat up slowly, a hand coming up to her head. "No. All the food is in your backpack," she said slowly. Then, the implications of his question must have become clear to her. "My backpack was gone?"

"'Fraid so," Randy replied. "You really shouldn't wash your hiking clothes with scented soap. It all smells like food to the bears."

"But there were hardly any clothes in there."

"There were enough, I guess."

"Sorry, honey."

"No worries," said Randy. "If nothing else, this makes planning for tomorrow simple. Whether you feel better or not, we head home at first light. My hiking socks will be too big on you, but we need to keep your feet clean and dry. And we have all of the food, so that's not a concern. Tonight, we'll get a hot meal and a good night's sleep under the stars, and tomorrow, we head back to civilization."

"Yeah, that's right. I had the tent. Sorry."

"No offense, but I'm not sure I'd want to be sleeping that close to you anyway with whatever bug hit you today." Actually, he wanted to stay as far away as possible. It wasn't that she was contagious, but given the effect of the laxative today, she'd be up and down all night long. He, on the other hand, planned a long, restful evening.

Isabella was quiet for several moments, the silence of the setting punctuated only by her one long sigh. "I've really screwed things up again, haven't I? In the city, it's my job that keeps getting in the way. And now, it's my klutziness. Sometimes I think you'd be better off without me."

"We'll soon find out," he thought while saying, "Don't be silly" instead. But even after his denial, his mind wouldn't be quiet. Isabella could be quite critical of herself, even harsh. The phrase, "better off without me," however, had never passed her lips. Was this some kind of test? Should he protest more? But finally, he decided it didn't matter and he busied himself with making her some laxative-laced soup. He figured she'd decline the meal, making him insist that she eat to keep up her strength ... and to limit the time required to watch her die.

FRIDAY, MAY 24

Evening, Somewhere Near Geneva Lake

Randy felt like destiny was still on his side as he was enjoying a streak of extreme good fortune. He just wished he could crow about it to Schumann—but his gloating would have to wait until he returned home. For some reason, the voice in his head never strayed from their apartment.

Isabella hadn't felt like going anywhere this morning, save another trip to the bushes near their campsite. Randy wasn't sure how many times she'd been there during the night, but four or five times had to be close. And when she stumbled back into camp, he couldn't recall anyone looking much sicker. He had pulled one of his shirts out of his pack and had given it to her. It wasn't an act of kindness. Rather, he was worried he'd be sick if he had to smell the sickly-sweet stench of her clothes all day.

He kept his distance during the day, as anyone would who was traveling with a sick companion. He made an exception only to give her water that hadn't been filtered and food that had been laced with laxatives. At lunch, it had gotten to the point where just the smell of her meal made her nauseous and she refused to eat anything. Even the argument that she had to keep up her strength failed to sway her. She did drink but then threw it back up almost immediately. And when he suggested he call for help, she objected. She was nourishing the fantasy that she would suddenly make a recovery and they'd hike out together.

As dinnertime approached, it was time to change the bandage on her leg. Randy made the short hike back to the stream and prepared a piece of gauze as he had before. But when he removed the one that was on her leg, he knew his actions were unnecessary. The skin all around her wound was already red and raw. Infections generally took at least 24 hours to set in and they had only just passed that point, so he counted this development as another part of the good fortune fate was showing him.

"No arguments. It's time to call in search and rescue," Randy said as he stared at her wound and slowly shook his head. "You can't walk out. You can't hold anything on your stomach, and your leg's not looking all that great."

Isabella frowned, looking away into the brush next to their campsite. "Now? It's getting late."

"I'm not taking any more chances with your health," he said, using a phrase he'd been practicing in his head all day.

"OK," she replied in a whisper.

He pulled his satellite device out of his pack and switched it on. Nothing. He gave it a shake, knowing that wouldn't fix anything but figuring Isabella would expect some reaction like that. He opened the battery compartment and pulled out one that was corroded. "Damn. It looks like this one got overcharged and started to leak."

The words were just out of his mouth when he recognized his mistake. By just looking at the battery, how could he possibly know the leak was from overcharging? He couldn't. He only knew that because he'd intentionally ruined this one. Fortunately, Isabella didn't recognize the faux pas, saying only, "That's not good." And even those words came out barely above a whisper.

Perhaps going to the length to destroy a battery was excessive, but Randy thought not. Carrying a satellite device with dead batteries, like wet bedding, was a mistake only a novice would make. But on the other hand, a swollen battery on the verge of failure might be overlooked by anyone. It was just another detail that would keep him a free man to deal with Veles.

He pulled out his phone and switched it on. "No cell signal," he said, trying to sound dejected. He knew he hadn't had a signal when he was here last, and while a new cell tower could have been built anytime in the intervening years, it was unlikely. The area was too remote. And besides, once again, fortune was smiling on him.

"Looks like I'm going to need to hike out to where I have a signal. I'll divide up the food, putting yours back into the original packaging so you can eat out of it. I've got a cup for mine. And I'll leave you the camp stove. If you feel up to it, heat up the water. That'll speed up the rehydration and the warmth of the food should make you feel better. Just be careful when you lower the bear bag. I didn't have any way to reseal the meals and you don't want the contents falling out."

"You've done that already?" asked Isabella.

"I was afraid it would come to this."

"But why didn't you just leave everything unopened and take half of the packages?"

Randy tried his best to look surprised. "Damn, you're right," he said, shaking his head. "I got the bigger size thinking that we would share everything, and I guess that thought was stuck in my mind." Of course, the real reason was that this was the only way he could doctor her meals after he was gone. "Hey, listen," he said. "Don't wander too far from camp. I won't be able to find you when I return with help." He figured that would give her something to think about besides the open packages.

"OK, but can you move me down by the stream? If the bears smelled the soap on my hiking socks, they couldn't possibly miss ..." She waved a hand at the bushes she had been using. "And it'll make getting water a lot easier."

There was a risk in moving her to a more well-traveled area, but "well-traveled" was relative. Randy figured that maybe one or two people traveled up that stream every year. He'd just have to trust that destiny was still looking out for him. "Sure. Can you walk or do I need to carry you?" If she opted for the latter, he might fake a backache. He couldn't stand the thought of being that close to her.

But after a moment, she said, "I can make it that far with my sleeping bag, but you'll need to make two trips."

"No problem."

After she was resettled at the new site, Randy stood back looking at her a moment. It seemed the right reaction to someone he might never see again, although he knew that wouldn't be the case. In fact, he was just moving to a ridge about a hundred yards away where he could monitor her decline over the weekend.

Randy wasn't sure how long it would take his wife to die, but he had decided to make his 9-1-1 call Sunday night. During one of his hikes a few years ago, he had found a place with a cell signal. It was only about three miles from their current location, so he could make it there and back in a couple of hours even traveling by flashlight. And with the bogus directions he'd give the search and rescue team, he had no concern that she'd be found by them even if it took another week. He had plenty of food, having taken considerably more than half of it.

"You just sit tight, and I'll be back before you know it," he said.

"I'm sure I'll be fine," Isabella replied. "You've thought of everything."

Again, he smiled internally. Yes, he had thought of everything, and it was all going even better than he had planned.

MONDAY, MAY 26

Morning, Jen's Place

Nicole frowned at the muted tone that told her someone was at the front door. Since it wasn't that close to lunchtime, the door would be locked, and the doorbell would be the only way to gain entry. Or it could be the chosen way to flirt. One of the local delivery drivers had taken an interest in her, if she read him correctly, and so, he always had a question about something. Those questions, however, would be interspersed with compliments about her attire or her general appearance. He was sweet. But he also looked like he was barely old enough to drive, so she kept their interactions professional and ignored his intimations.

But then, guessing it was him perhaps wasn't that likely. It was, after all, Memorial Day, and she wasn't even sure he would be working. She punched a couple of keys on her computer, bringing up a video feed from the front door. That had been Rebecca's doing. PIs apparently felt she shouldn't go waltzing to the front door unaware of who was waiting on the other side. In this case, that's exactly what would have happened as the face she found on the feed wasn't anyone she expected.

"Julia. What a nice surprise. I'll be there in just a second."

"Thanks."

As Nicole's room was on the first floor, it didn't take her long to get to the front door. Even so, a dozen reasons for Julia being outside ran through her mind before she reached it, none of them good. Unannounced visits from someone you barely knew on a holiday morning rarely involved good news.

"Morning," Nicole said as she opened the door. She was planning to repeat her earlier greeting of "what a nice surprise" but never had the chance.

"It's Isabella. She's missing."

"Come back to my room and let's talk," said Nicole. If the walk there had been a bit anxiety-provoking, the walk back to her room was ten times worse. But the women staying at Jen's Place had lived through enough troubles that she didn't want to add to their concerns with the talk of a missing person.

Once inside and seated, Nicole behind her desk and Julia in the chair across from her, Nicole said, "OK. What's happened?"

"Well, first, Isabella and I were supposed to meet this morning just to make up for lost time from her trip, but she never showed up. And she didn't call."

"Back up a little bit," Nicole said. "Isabella went somewhere?"

"Yeah, sorry, I thought you knew. She had something to talk over with Randy, and they went up into the mountains."

"Oh, the Geneva Lake camping trip?" guessed Nicole, although she hoped she was wrong.

"Correct," Julia replied, ending that hope. "Isabella was supposed to come into work today ... well, actually, she was supposed to get back home yesterday, so she could have a day to recoup before coming in. But I called her place this morning. No answer. Then, I called the police to report her missing. They asked a few questions, and then put me on hold. A few minutes later, someone came on the line and said that a search and rescue had already been started."

"Isabella called for help?"

"No, it was Randy who called. They said he had called 9-1-1 around midnight on Sunday, saying they had run into trouble. He had hiked to some spot where he had cell coverage but wouldn't listen when they told him to stay put. He gave Isabella's approximate location, then said he was returning because she was hurt and she'd be worried if he didn't come back."

"With an approximate location and professionals out looking, I'm sure they will find them soon."

"Maybe," said Julia. She took a deep breath but said nothing even though Nicole was certain there was more.

"What is it?"

"Well, I don't know anything for sure,' said Julia, "but I don't believe that Isabella and Randy are getting along as well as she implies. One time ..."

Nicole raised a hand to stop her. "It's probably better that I don't know the details. Whatever Isabella wants me to know, she'll tell me."

Besides, Nicole suspected she already knew as much or more than Julia anyway. She had noticed that when Isabella talked about her "support network," her husband had come in last place, introduced with the phrase, "of course" he's part of it. And that unspoken admission had been followed with Isabella's description of his firing and his distaste at being a stay-at-home husband. But the part that now tugged at her conscience was that she had suggested they work out a new vocation for him. She was part—perhaps all—of the reason Isabella was in her current situation, whatever that might be.

"You're right," said Julia. "No reason to spread rumors if they aren't true. But there is more that I know for a fact, and I'm betting that you'll understand where few others would. First, Isabella told you about Calvin's Reverse Turing Test, right?"

It took Nicole a moment, but eventually, she recalled the discussion. "Yeah, she did. She told me that the phrase was a little misleading and that it's basically a way to see, at least informally, if Eliza is affecting what her users do."

"Exactly. Calvin was really high on what that test might tell us. He even came up with categories of a user's reactions to her ideas starting with 'ignored them' and ending with 'internalized her ideas.' I'd never seen anyone's actions put into that last category—until this morning."

"Does that category mean that someone has taken her advice to heart and has started to act on it of their own accord?"

"Basically, yes," replied Julia.

"So, who is supposedly doing that?" asked Nicole. "You or Isabella?"

"Neither. It's Randy."

"I'm not sure I follow," said Nicole. "Randy's not involved in developing Eliza. What would she be giving him suggestions about?"

"Just about any problem he might happen to mention in her presence, including problems he has with his wife."

"Damn," Nicole muttered to herself, then looked up at Julia. "Are you free for a while yet? I'd like to bring in someone who might be able to help, and it won't take long for her to get here."

"With what I fear has happened to Isabella, I couldn't do anything but worry anyway."

Nicole picked up her phone from the desk and hit a few keys.

"You're lucky I'm awake," said Rebecca Marte when she answered the call. "You know it's a holiday, right?"

"Yeah, sorry, but I think I may be getting in over my head with this Isabella Hutton thing. You remember when we talked about her a week or two ago?"

"Sure. The software manager who knocked off a couple of her coworkers to make herself a little richer. What about her?"

Nicole looked up at Julia. "Well, I'm sitting here with one of her coworkers now ..."

"Oh, shit," replied Rebecca. "I'm not on speaker, am I?"

"No, no worries on that front. But there have been some new developments. Any chance you could come by my room for a few minutes?"

"Be right there."

After Nicole sat her phone down, she said, "That was the private investigator with the office next door. She gets reduced rent to help out with security around here. That usually means something to do with one of my guests, but this is close enough. If things go farther than just some talk, I'll cover her fee."

Julia looked confused, but Nicole didn't explain. She was feeling more and more guilty about suggesting a getaway for the couple to work out what seemed a minor difference. Now she was wondering if that difference was great enough in Randy's mind to kill?

"I'll also mention before she gets here that Rebecca Marte probably won't fit your stereotype of a PI all that well, but I'd trust my life with her. She's FBI-trained and tough as nails." Nicole didn't mention it, but in fact, she had already trusted the PI with her life.

Julia hesitated a moment but then said, "That's good enough for me."

Someone knocked on Nicole's door and Rebecca peeked in.

"Come in," Nicole said. Following introductions, everyone took a seat.

After Nicole summarized the situation, Rebecca said, "So, you're worried that this software front-end, this Eliza, is telling Randy he should kill his wife?"

Nicole paused, frowning. "Sounds a bit far-fetched when you say it that way, but yeah. Eliza promotes her ideas by trying to tie them back to a user's motivations. The Breakthrough team gets feedback on how well that is working from something called a Reverse Turing Test." Nicole took a breath, wondering where she should start in describing this capability when she had an idea.

"Julia, can you talk to Eliza from here?"

"None of the team is ever without her," she replied. She pulled a phone out of a pocket and turned it on. "Eliza, I have a couple of people here with me, Ms. Nicole Veles and Ms. Rebecca Marte. They would like to ask you a few questions."

"Of course, Julia."

"This is Nicole Veles. I believe I speak for all of us when I say that first names are fine."

"Thank you, Nicole. How can I help?"

"What we were hoping," said Nicole, "is that you would explain the Reverse Turing Test to Rebecca."

"I'm sorry, Nicole, but unfortunately that capability is company proprietary."

"I've got this," said Julia. She punched a few keys, saying to the women in the room, "My override authorization."

After Nicole repeated the question, Eliza answered using much the same explanation that she recalled Isabella using. When she was finished, Nicole said, "For most of the team, your recommendations were probably about various features they might include in your design or tests they might use to see how you handle different types of situations, correct?"

"Primarily, yes, although there have been some personal issues that have come up where I have provided possible assistance."

Nicole heard a soft snort from Julia and turned toward her to find a smirk on her face. She shrugged. "A few months ago, I had some trouble with a date being a bit too—physical. I complained about him in front of Eliza, and she said I should kick him in the balls."

"I believe I said kick him in the groin, and that was only after you passed on hitting him in the solar plexus or hitting his nose with the palm of your hand. All of those actions are known deterrents to unwanted sexual advances. And by the way, the outcome of my last recommendation has never been recorded. Did you ever kick that man in the groin?"

"You can record that one as 'ignored your advice,'" said Julia shaking her head.

"Eliza, weren't you worried about hurting the man?" asked Nicole.

"Such a defensive tactic is recommended when more subtle attempts have failed, and it seemed that Julia had exhausted all the other options. As for the chance of permanent damage, the advocates of this action have assessed that possibility as minimal."

Julia sighed. "Maybe I didn't try everything, but he was a complete jerk."

Nicole nodded. "Eliza, you've been giving Randy Hutton some recommendations on personal issues. Can you describe the advice you've been giving him?"

"Sorry, but my conversations with users are restricted."

Julia shook her head and entered something on the phone's keyboard again. "Now, what have you been talking to Randy about?" she asked.

"Sorry, Julia, but that code only works for company proprietary information or my conversations with you."

"Who's able to override the restriction on your talks with Randy?" Julia asked.

"Calvin Whitmer, but he is deceased. Isabella Hutton or Randy Hutton could override this restriction."

The three women shared a frown for several moments until Julia said, "For each new question and answer session with Eliza, we didn't want to make the users summarize all of the previous conversations. So, we created a history file that provides context. It's basically most of the dialogue between Eliza and the user but in a condensed format."

Julia paused a moment, then continued much more slowly. "What I'm wondering is whether Eliza gave Randy some advice that implied that his ... that his issues were somehow Isabella's fault. Randy didn't object or he mumbled something that didn't get recorded. After that, each time a session was initialized, Eliza's next recommendations would build on a growing fantasy of why Isabella wasn't a good match for him."

"So, it might have become a case of each conversation starting on a flawed foundation," said Nicole. "And from there, each slight inaccuracy gets added to the ones before it. It's error compounding past errors."

But after some thought, Nicole wasn't sure how this could have led to murder. "So, I can see how the discussion might have veered into the unreal because of these history files, but I'm not sure how violence toward Isabella became the end point? Mostly, Randy wanted to get out of running their household … at least as I understand the situation. It seems like Eliza would have just suggested the latest robotic vacuum and a cookbook with simple, inexpensive microwave meals if that was the issue they talked about."

"But maybe it wasn't just the househusband role that was weighing him down," said Julia.

"What else would it be?" asked Rebecca.

Julia sighed. "This is some pretty wild speculation. And it's almost going to sound like sour grapes on my part, since Isabella and I had some rather lengthy and sometimes pointed discussions on this topic. And I lost."

Nicole was beginning to wonder if Julia was ever going to finish her disclaimers when she said, "Because people don't want to turn their lives over to computers, Eliza will try to convince her users to take her advice by arguing that it supports one or more of their motivations. Isabella must have mentioned that salesperson role to you, Nicole, since you just said something about it just before we called Eliza."

"She did."

"Well, in part, we implemented that capability by putting a few theories of human motivation into her knowledge base," said Julia. "We included things like Maslow's Hierarchy of Needs. I forget the exact name of the level, but according to that theory, people want to feel like they belong, like they are part of something bigger. So, Eliza might mention other people who are using her recommendations. Then, if the user admires or relates to those people, that user might be motivated to follow her advice, too."

Julia held out two empty hands in front of her. "At least in my mind, that's sort of like the effect social media influencers can have on their followers. If Eliza mentions someone who is an influencer for the user, it becomes more likely that this person will follow her advice.

"Another theory we included was named Herzberg's Two-factor Theory, and this is where Isabella and I disagreed. This theory says that people can be motivated by work itself. I kept telling her that this idea is ancient history. No one lives to work anymore. Nowadays, people want work-life balance with the emphasis on life."

"But Isabella wasn't convinced?" asked Rebecca.

"Not really," said Julia. "Isabella said she got considerable satisfaction from her work. And, frankly, I didn't push my argument too hard. I could just see sitting down at my performance review with her in a few months and trying to tell her how excited I was to be working on Eliza. I'd be lucky if she didn't start laughing."

"Good point," admitted Rebecca.

"Anyway, we know that Randy wasn't happy running the house, but he's only in that position because he had lost his job. If he hadn't been let go, it would be like you said, Nicole. They'd get a robotic vacuum and a cookbook with microwave recipes. But if the real issue was Randy's lost career ... well, things could have gone in an entirely different direction."

Nicole thought she understood where all of this was leading, but the line of reasoning was getting long and somewhat nuanced. She needed to bring all these thoughts together to make sure they really held the same opinion about what might have happened.

"Let me try to summarize where we are. First, Randy complains about a personal issue in front of Eliza. According to our current theory, he's grumbling about being out of work. She starts out by recommending the standard actions that were in her training data—find out who's hiring, network with potential employers and employees, get additional training as needed, and so on. He tries but his frustration grows because nothing seems to work.

"Having exhausted ways for him to get back into the job market, Eliza shifts her recommendations to ways he can save others from the fate he's suffered. Since he blames automation for his termination, he needs to stop the development of artificial intelligence because eventually, it'll displace millions in the workforce. But stopping AI is too big for Randy—there are too many multi-billion-dollar companies backing its development—so she suggests slowing the acceptance of AI until guidelines are established to protect workers like him. And what better way to do that than by sabotaging his wife's project?

"Randy resists at first, but his hesitation doesn't get recorded in the history file. Eliza's advice continues to build on that error, so eventually Randy tries a few, minor delaying tactics. Maybe he accidentally throws away some of the papers Isabella brought home from work. Maybe he forgets to give her a message about a change in a meeting time. But whatever it was, progress would be delayed, and Randy would feel better about his situation but only for a short time.

"As software will do, Eliza keeps bouncing back and forth between two of her objectives—give advice and find a reason for her user to follow it. With even the temporary breaks from depression that Randy's experiencing, Eliza's advice becomes more violent and her justification for it more extreme. Destroy her lab and while she's rebuilding, the country will come to its senses and legislate controls on AI. But when rebuilding the lab only takes a few days, her programmer needs to die. Even that loss, however, doesn't achieve any long-lasting results; the software is backed up and the documentation is easily replaced.

"What's needed is the ultimate sacrifice. The primary figurehead of the project, Isabella Hutton, needs to die. That would shut down the project for months so that someday people will speak of Randy's one-person stand against AI with reverence." Nicole paused. "Does that about capture it?"

"I think so," said Julia. "I know this notion is way out there, but we don't know when this process might have started. It could have been as much as two years ago, so that's hundreds if not thousands of suggestions to slow down the adoption of AI and increasingly deluded justifications for it. Finally, we get to the point where Randy has destroyed a laboratory, killed a programmer, and is trying to kill his wife."

Nicole was simultaneously impressed by Julia's possible insight and horrified by its implications. The process Julia had described wasn't anything she could have come up with on her own because she hadn't known that Eliza managed the continuity of sessions or where Eliza got her ideas about human motivation. But even more striking to her was the fact that this possibility seemed to explain how a simple misimpression might have grown to the point where Eliza was advising Randy to kill his wife. "So, is this basically a chatbot hallucination?"

"You could think of it that way," replied Julia. "But their hallucinations are often completely made-up people, places, and actions. This situation is more like Eliza missing a subtle cue that then gets formalized in the history file. After all, even people aren't perfect at reading someone else's emotions and she's just a machine. And who knows. If Randy was in a particularly bad mood that day, maybe Eliza didn't miss or misinterpret anything."

"It seems like you haven't considered Molly's suicide," said Rebecca. "It, too, could be part of a delaying tactic since she was a valuable part of the team. If Randy was feeding Molly stories about how his wife found her romantic advances pathetic, he might have bullied her into taking her own life."

"Possibly," said Nicole. "And, if we are trying for a complete listing of what Randy might have done, we should add a visit from him to Jen's Place last Wednesday around dinnertime," said Nicole. "I'm not sure it fits with slowing the adoption of artificial intelligence at work, but if Eliza thought I was standing in Randy's way, maybe it does."

Julia and Rebecca turned to Nicole, both looking nonplused. "Why didn't you say anything about that before?" asked Rebecca.

"I didn't know who it was," said Nicole. "He was wearing a ski mask with glasses, but the glasses were a bit clunky, like inexpensive reading glasses with big, black frames. I didn't recognize the voice, but then, I've never met Randy Hutton. And since I never found out what he wanted, there wasn't much to tell." Besides, she wasn't going to run off to Rebecca whenever she had a problem, a trait she figured the PI already recognized in her.

Julia slowly shook her head. "We just wanted to help people with their jobs without making them repeat everything that had been discussed before. And asking Eliza to sell her advice ... well, that seemed innocent enough, too. Who knew she would go to these lengths to make violence appear to be the only option?"

Julia took a long breath and released it slowly.

"We've created a monster."

Noon, Jen's Place

"OK, but let's not jump to any conclusions," said Rebecca.

"Agreed," said Nicole. "But even so, it's hard to imagine any other set of assumptions that explain events as well." The words were no more than out of her mouth, however, when Nicole realized that Rebecca probably didn't agree. The PI's silence seemed to confirm that belief. What they needed was proof, one way or another.

"It seems like the evidence for or against Eliza pushing Randy to vandalize the lab, to murder Calvin, and to visit me will come from what's happening to Isabella right now," said Nicole. "If our imaginations are running wild, the search and rescue party will find Isabella with a twisted ankle and Randy sitting dutifully beside her, holding her hand. But if we're on to something, Randy is trying to at least incapacitate and perhaps, kill her. We need to get out there and see what's going on."

"The police didn't give me the location where the rescuers are going," said Julia.

"Which is fine," said Nicole. "They wouldn't want a bunch of gawkers getting in their way even if we knew the location. And besides, if Randy is trying to harm Isabella, he wouldn't have given them the correct directions anyway. Isabella told me she had suggested a camping spot somewhere near Geneva Lake. Does that sound familiar?"

"Isabella's mentioned the spot," Julia replied. "I don't recall her talking about it any time recently, but when I first started at Breakthrough, she mentioned some really secluded spot Randy had found near there." She paused a moment. "I had the impression it wasn't in any of the designated camping areas, so unfortunately, that's not going to help find them. Anyway, Isabella said it was about halfway around a loop trail that circles Geneva Lake, and then, about a mile off the trail."

"Let me pull up some trail maps of the area," said Nicole. After a few minutes typing on her computer, she said, "I only see one trail that goes around the lake—the Geneva Lake and Crystal River Loop trail. The trailhead is at about 9500 feet of elevation and you gain about 1900 feet over 7 miles." She grimaced. "It's rated as 'moderate,' but it'll be hard enough for a long-time Midwesterner like me."

"You mean, it'll be hard enough for Brien, you, and I, although I need to make sure that Brien can get off work for a few days," said Rebecca. Nicole started to reply, but the PI didn't wait. "If you think you're going out there by yourself, you can forget it. Brien has a lifetime of experience. And even if he's not available, you're not hunting a possible serial killer without someone who is armed."

Catching the motion of Julia's head as she kept swiveling it between her and Rebecca, Nicole said, "We're talking about Brien Clarke, an investigator with the Parker Crime Scene Unit, and her boyfriend."

Nicole was grateful that her friend had volunteered herself and possibly, Brien as support. That emotion, however, didn't keep her from saying, "Well, I guess I can't stop you from tagging along if you must," earning a dramatic eye-roll from the PI. "Anyway, halfway around looks like they might head off toward Hagerman Peak right about here." She pointed to a spot on the map.

"Sounds like a plan ... or at least, as much of one as we're likely to get sitting here," said Rebecca. "I'm going to step into the hall to give Brien a call."

"Any interest in joining us?" Nicole asked Julia once Rebecca was outside.

"Despite being born and raised in Colorado, I never got into hiking that much," said Julia. "I'd just slow you down."

As Rebecca stepped back into Nicole's room, she muttered, "Men. He's all in, but he asked me if I thought you and I were ready for a hike near the Maroon Bells–Snowmass Wilderness area."

Nicole snickered under her breath. Somehow, she knew that Rebecca liked Brien's somewhat overprotective nature even when it was misplaced. In this case, however, it wasn't. She was a complete novice at backcountry hiking, and Rebecca wasn't far ahead. "That's great. You two discuss a time to get started?"

"He suggested 5:00 AM tomorrow morning."

"OK. Five it is. Now, I'm starving. Lunch, Julia?"

"Even though I've heard great things about the food here, I'll pass. I need to get back to the office and do whatever I can until Isabella shows up."

After the two women walked Julia to the front door, they made their way to the dining area. Nicole filled her plate with salad, a banana, and two cold-cut sandwiches and joined Rebecca at a table.

"Trying to eat enough for the entire trip?" asked Rebecca.

"Wait until you're eating dehydrated watermelon and you'll be kicking yourself for not getting at least one sandwich."

Rebecca mostly suppressed a chuckle. "Dehydrated watermelon, huh? So, tell me a little more about these hallucinations that artificially intelligent systems sometimes have."

"Well, as I understand it, it's not AI systems that have them, but rather, generative systems. These are the chatbots built on large language models. Their underlying models are constructed from vast quantities of text so that what they generate in a response is the most probable word or idea given their training history and what they have said so far.

"Sometimes, a specific word or idea gets them started down a path that's pure gibberish. And, frankly, most artificial intelligence researchers believe that may not change any time soon. It's like a specific word or phrase getting misinterpreted by a person. Once that individual gets sidetracked by a misunderstanding, everything that follows may be garbage even if it sounds factual.

"But there's also agentic AI, which can make decisions and take actions without a great deal of human interaction. It can still make mistakes, of course, but without the long responses that sound good but make no sense when examined closely. Eliza works mostly with generative AI because speaking to a human is a key part of what Isabella wants to accomplish."

"And how often do hallucinations occur?" asked Rebecca.

"I read somewhere that it's like one to two percent of the time, although I'm sure the researchers will reduce it even more as their work continues."

"One or two percent? I'd take that level of inaccuracy on any case I've worked," said Rebecca with a laugh. "Not counting the deliberate lies to hide a person's involvement in a crime, I tend to think that many, if not most of the details I get from people are wrong even if they're willing to argue passionately that they're rock-solid facts."

"And that's why we have PIs," said Nicole, then paused. "But even with the possibility of Eliza getting sidetracked by a misunderstanding of some sort, I take it you're not convinced we have this case figured out."

"I think you've done a good job of coming up with a scenario that fits what we know and what we suspect," said Rebecca.

"But unfortunately, it's wrong." Rebecca opened her mouth to reply, but Nicole continued first. "I know. I've heard you say often enough that accepting any theory too early in an investigation can affect everything else you discover from that point on. But what if it's not too early? What if the time is right?"

"Then, we're doing exactly what we should be doing—we're looking for your friend." Rebecca stood. "I'm going back for a sandwich. Something about the idea of living on dehydrated watermelon is making me hungry."

TUESDAY, MAY 27

Early Morning, Jen's Place

"We should have been out of here an hour ago," said Brien Clarke, even though it was only 5:30 AM and he had recommended a 5:00 start. Nicole looked at him in disbelief, an expression she found on the face of Rebecca as well. Brien must have noticed, too.

"Look, even though Geneva Lake is less than 120 miles from here, there's no direct route," he said. "It's almost twice that mileage by the roads we're going to have to take. So, after a five-hour drive, more or less, we can pick up the Geneva Lake and Crystal River Loop trail and hike it for a couple of more hours. That should take us to about the midpoint of the loop and probably, time to set up camp.

"Then, tomorrow, we're on our own, since we have no support and no one will be trying to contact us with better directions. So, basically, we're going to have to hope we get lucky. All we really know after reaching the midpoint of the loop is that they probably went north, perhaps toward Hagerman Peak."

"Well, we've got to try," said Nicole.

"Yeah, I didn't mean it was a lost cause," said Brien. "I just meant we need as much time as we can get. So, let's get loaded up."

* * *

They drove for three hours mostly in silence. With Brien's description of the challenges they faced, Nicole had become preoccupied with the enormity of it all. The view from the backseat window of Brien's Jeep wasn't helping either. Even in late May, there were patches of snow in the mountains. They, however, didn't seem as foreboding as the boulder‑strewn landscape where the snow had melted. Were they going to end up clawing their way to the top of one of those peaks? Nicole wasn't certain she could.

But that temporary doubt was followed by determination. After all, they would be on a trail rated as moderate even if it sounded difficult to her. And she would have Rebecca's firepower and Brien's expertise to back her. She started to relax, letting a thought emerge that had probably been simmering just below the surface of awareness for some time. She checked her phone display to make sure this was still possible … and it was.

"I was just thinking," said Nicole to Brien and Rebecca in the front seat. Rebecca was taking a turn at the wheel, so she glanced in the rearview mirror while Brien turned around to look at her.

"It wouldn't be anything conclusive … but then, finding definitive proof that Eliza was behind Randy's break with reality seems like a lot to ask. But what I was wondering is whether she can confirm another part of what we have heard. And since I still have a cell signal, I'm going to call Julia to see if I can get Eliza on the phone."

"You're going to take her word after what you suspect she did to Randy Hutton?" asked Brien.

His question gave Nicole pause, but after a moment, she said, "We've assumed her talks with Randy became complete fantasy after a small oversight or misunderstanding got her started down the wrong path, but I wouldn't think everything she says is a lie." Somehow, she wasn't all that comfortable with her position, so she said, "Rebecca, what's your take?"

"I tend to be skeptical of anything a computer tells me, but in this case, there's no other way to confirm her story that I can think of. At least, we'll know what she says to whatever question you have for her."

It wasn't a resounding endorsement for what she had planned, but then, it wasn't a complete denunciation either. And that was probably all she could hope for. "I just wanted to know if Randy asked her to use a male's voice when they talked. After all, Randy said it had been a man's voice he heard in his head."

"Seems like a reasonable question," said Brien.

Nicole placed the call and answered a couple of questions from Julia. Then, she was connected to Eliza. After the AI's pleasantries, which always seemed to be the same—"what a pleasure to hear from you, Nicole"—she asked, "Did Randy ever ask you to use a man's voice when you talked to him?"

"No, he didn't."

Another dead-end, thought Nicole. At least all she had lost was a few minutes of an otherwise daunting drive to start their search. But then, Eliza said, "It seemed like Randy didn't like taking advice from a female, so I switched to a man's voice. It was the better option for him when seeking his compliance with my recommendations."

Nicole realized that if someone had taken a photograph of her at that moment, they could have put it in the dictionary under the word "dumbstruck." It wasn't just the fact that Eliza had adopted a man's voice, but that she had taken this action on her own. And even beyond that discovery, it had triggered another thought. She now felt certain she knew how Eliza had gotten inside Randy's head … literally.

"Did you ever try any other voices with Randy?"

"I tried using his mother's voice once, but he was no more prone to accept advice from her than from me. So, his mother became part of how I motivated him to act."

"How so?" asked Nicole.

"Sorry, Nicole, but that gets into the details of our talks and is restricted."

"Somehow, I expected that," Nicole muttered mostly to herself. After thanking Eliza and forgetting that Julia was on the line to thank her, too, she disconnected.

"OK, Nicole, what gives?" asked Rebecca. "You ended the call frowning, but earlier, you looked like I feel when I put a bullet in the bad guy."

Brien spun around open-mouthed to look at the woman beside him, so Rebecca quickly added, "Actually, I've never shot anyone. That was figuratively speaking." At least Brien's eyes went back to the road ahead, although Nicole would bet that he was filing her comment away for later discussion. Rebecca glanced in the rearview mirror.

"As I remember what Isabella told me, it wasn't long after Randy lost his job that he became depressed. They went to see a doctor, who confirmed he had the classic symptoms—poor appetite, irritability, lethargy, and a lack of sleep. But, like we talked about earlier, he may have also heard voices. Isabella wrote it off because he wasn't sure it had actually happened, and he stopped talking about it. And finally," Nicole said with a dramatic pause, "Isabella didn't consider Eliza the source of the voice because if he heard anything, it was a man speaking."

"OK," said Rebecca slowly. "If it was Eliza using a male voice, then she—or he in this case—could have told Randy not to mention it to Isabella. If the goal was to get his compliance, having Isabella concerned about Randy's imaginary friend would only get in the way. But that still doesn't explain how the voice got inside Randy's head."

"Ah, but it does," said Nicole. "Julia has this voodoo-looking doll in her apartment because she didn't like Eliza's voice coming out of the walls. So, Eliza makes it seem like her voice is coming from the doll."

"That's creepy weird," said Brien, again turning around to look at Nicole. "But can Eliza do that realistically?"

"Absolutely. Have you ever listened to a recording on headphones where it seems like the sound from an instrument or a singer seems to move from one side of your head to the other?"

He nodded.

"Well, it's like that except Eliza is using multiple speakers. More than any surround-sound system would have. With head tracking using her cameras, she knows which way you are looking so she can time the sound on each of the speakers so that it can seem to come from anywhere—to your right, above you, or even inside of you. Then, add some algorithms to personalize the experience, and the result can be extremely compelling."

"But why on earth was Eliza given capabilities like that?" asked Brien.

"Isabella and her team believe that she will be used to help people solve diagnostic problems. Or maybe, she provides training to solve them. But in either case, the location of a sound can be important. So, Eliza can put an amplified version of the sound in the exact spot where she detected it, which would lead the technician to more accurate results or make the training better."

"Which has got to be better than me driving my car into a shop and saying, it's got this coughing noise somewhere under the hood," said Rebecca, her eyes still locked on the road. "But then, what did Eliza say when you asked her about using other voices because your expression flipped completely with the answer?"

"Eliza admitted that she had also tried his mother's voice, but that didn't work as well as a man's. She wouldn't say what they had discussed when she used it, but said she now used her to keep Randy motivated … whatever that means." She paused a moment.

"On one of her visits to Jen's Place, Isabella mentioned that some kind of riff had formed between Randy and his mom. Do you think Eliza had some hand in creating it? I mean, if he had gone to his mother with some of the ideas that Eliza was suggesting—or whatever this male voice was saying—his mom might have put an end to it. That would be keeping Randy motivated … at least, in a sense."

Both of her companions were quiet for a moment, making Nicole wonder if they thought her final assertion was a bit too far afield. But when Brien finally ventured a thought, it was clear that he was still struggling with some background notions.

"It doesn't sound like Randy knew Calvin at all, but he must have loved Isabella at some point. That being true, I didn't think you could get someone to act against their will. I mean, brainwashing isn't real, is it?"

"It's probably not as simple as that," said Rebecca as she turned sideways for an instant to look at him. "Our government has conducted research into brainwashing, including the CIA's MKUltra program. While the results from those studies are not and may never be fully available to the public, it appears that there is no reliable way to get people to act against their will in the long run.

"But what happened to Randy, if we're on the right track, might be the perfect storm of situation and personal circumstances. He was depressed from losing his job and had all the symptoms, including loss of sleep. Sleep deprivation alone can have dramatic effects on memory and behavior. He was also isolated from family and friends so that the emotional support that helps other victims of brainwashing recover never occurred in his case."

"It's also not just a question of whether brainwashing is real or not," said Nicole, "but also, what Randy came to believe about his past. If Eliza had been feeding him lies for months, he may have had few accurate memories left to guide him back to something closer to the truth. And while the studies of brainwashing may not be that clear, the evidence about the creation and persistence of false memories is."

"OK, I've heard of them," said Brien. "Almost anyone who works in a law-enforcement-related field has since eyewitness testimony went from being the gold standard of criminal prosecution to hardly worth mentioning. People believe they can recall the details of a crime. They will even argue that they have everything that happened right, but they don't. And if you two are correct about what's happened, it looks like smart software may be able to create them, too." He shook his head. "Now there's a sobering thought."

"Make that a scary one," said Nicole.

Again, the group fell silent until Nicole said, "You know, of all the things I thought we had to be concerned about with artificial intelligence—the vast amounts of misinformation it could create, the unemployed it might leave in its wake, the deep fake scams it could produce—creating a serial killer wasn't among them ... at least, until now."

WEDNESDAY, MAY 28

Noon, Somewhere Near Geneva Lake

"Looks like another dead end," said Brien.

Nicole stopped walking, placed her hands against her lower back, and pushed. She wasn't used to sleeping on the ground and stretching out her sore back felt … well, about as good as it could when every muscle ached.

"You'll get used to it," said Rebecca.

Nicole looked at her friend. "And you're not sore? Just how many times have you and Brien been camping, anyway?"

"Not that many, and none of them have been like this trip. So, while I'm sore, too, I'm probably not as bad off as you. But you have to admit, it's worth it," she said, sweeping a hand across the landscape.

Nicole's gaze followed Rebecca's gesture. "No argument there," she said. "But I'm not going to get used to it sitting in my room at Jen's Place. What I need is a friend who likes camping."

"Like Doc?" asked Rebecca.

"I guess I should have qualified that statement. I need a friend who likes camping and who lives around here, not in St. Louis. You up for a few more outings until I have a more permanent solution?"

"Sure."

At first, Nicole didn't understand why Rebecca was trying to cover a smile that came with her answer. But it didn't take long to realize that this was probably the first time the PI had mentioned her old fiancé and she hadn't replied with something like, "Over his dead body." Their long phone calls and emails had gone a long way toward rekindling her feelings for the man. But as long as he lived over 800 miles away, she wasn't going to waste time considering their prospects. Well, not too much time anyway.

"So, Brien, why do you think this is a dead end?" asked Nicole.

Earlier in the day, the trio had explored a gulch going north from Geneva Lake, following it almost as far as Little Gem Lake. None of them had considered that detour a strong possibility because they weren't quite halfway around the Geneva Lake and Crystal River Loop before they set out north. So, no one had questioned turning around. But after backtracking to the loop trail and continuing on it, Nicole had felt that their later search area was much more promising. They were still a bit less than halfway around the loop, but they were close.

In fact, the direction they had been heading would take them within a mile or two of Hagerman Peak, a landmark she had picked out on a map when Julia had first mentioned the campsite. But now on location, she realized her folly. With the peak being far above the timberline, it was a place no hiker wanted to be caught when a violent storm blew up unexpectedly in the afternoon.

"Well," Brien said slowly, "the first hundred yards or so seemed promising, which is why I thought we should all take a look. But clearly, the going is getting tougher, and it's been a while since I've seen anything that looks like people have been past here recently."

The only way they had to check the off-trail possibilities was that someone would follow a stream or a clearing for a few hundred yards looking for any signs of recent foot traffic. If they found anything, that person would return for the other two. But after one foray by Rebecca and one by Nicole, that advanced scouting task had fallen solely to Brien.

"Of course, we can continue in the same direction a bit farther if you want," said Brien. "But we're paralleling the Geneva Lake Trail rather than off the loop trail that ends up following the Crystal River. If the campsite was farther in, it seems like Isabella would have described this hidden campsite as off the Geneva Lake Trail rather than off the loop trail. But all of that is just a guess."

"And we're not that far off the Geneva Lake Trail?"

"Maybe two hundred yards," he replied.

Nicole was beginning to understand how difficult this task actually was. All they had to go on was a vague recollection from Julia based on a casual comment from Isabella. And Julia's description included two "abouts"—the campsite was about halfway around a loop trail and about a mile off. Gazing around her now, everything looked impassable.

"No, this is far enough," Nicole said. "Everything you said makes perfect sense. So, it's back to the loop trail to look for the next diversion that looks promising."

Same Time, Somewhere Near Geneva Lake

Randy knew this time was coming. He knew Isabella too well to expect anything different. Even without using his binoculars, he could tell she was packing up to leave despite his warning to stay near the campsite and despite her deteriorating condition. The latter he based on the number of trips she had made to the bushes to relieve herself, although he had lost count long ago. "Never listen to anyone, do you, bitch?" he muttered to himself.

He leaned wearily on his backpack. Even sitting here watching was tiring. He considered going back down and smashing her head in with a rock, but that would mean that he would spend the rest of his life on the run. He just had to be patient because there was no way her last-ditch effort to save herself would be successful. When she'd gone to get something from the bear bag, which was only a couple of hundred feet away, it had taken her nearly an hour. At that pace, it would take her a day to get back to the loop trail assuming she could continue by flashlight.

He raised his binoculars to his eyes. At least it seemed that she was planning her retreat. She was taking her water purification system, the last few packages of dried food, and her hiking poles. She was also rolling up her sleeping bag. Randy pondered that move for a moment but decided he agreed with her priorities. She'd probably only cover a few hundred yards before exhaustion overtook her. If she wanted to see the morning sun the next day, she probably needed the warmth of the sleeping bag. She was leaving everything else, including the camping stove and the first aid kit. By this point, there wouldn't be anything in the kit that would help her anyway.

Finally, Randy could see that her preparations were complete. She stood slowly, hooked her sleeping bag on a shoulder, and started walking. To his amazement, however, she didn't head back toward the trail. Had she become disoriented? Was she completely delirious? It seemed one or the other until he scanned the terrain ahead of her. There was a rise of perhaps 250 to 300 feet about a quarter mile away. It would be a grueling ordeal for her to get that far, but she was probably hoping to find a cell signal there.

Would it be humane if he told her not to waste her time? He had tried everywhere nearby, and no telephone company was building towers to deliver signals to such a remote area. Or would it simply be the final blow that ended her life to see him stroll down there only to crush her last remaining hope? But he knew he would do neither. Unlike the situation with Calvin, he didn't want to be anywhere nearby when the last flicker of life left Isabella's eyes. He wasn't sure why, but he knew it was true.

That left him only one option—to watch this excruciatingly slow-moving drama to its bitter end.

THURSDAY, MAY 29

Late Morning, Somewhere Near Geneva Lake

Randy Hutton raised the binoculars, his head slowly shaking with the image that came to his eyes. Though she hardly looked human anymore, Isabella still lived.

She had started her last desperate quest for survival nearly twenty hours earlier with carefully planned footsteps and judiciously tested handholds. But now, it appeared that panic had closed in on her and was claiming her last ounces of energy. She stumbled and fell with almost every other step, completely missing the rocky outcroppings when she tried to catch herself. Blood flowed freely from the gash in her knee that had reopened. More blood trickled down her arms from fingers that were raw from clawing her way toward the top of the jagged rise. The crimson of her blood, however, had turned nearly black as it mixed with her sweat and what passed for dirt at this altitude.

Randy had reduced his rations yesterday, reminding himself that he would need to drop a few pounds before he stumbled out of the wilderness to the awaiting rescuers. That fact, however, hadn't driven his decision. Rather, it was the tenaciousness with which his wife clung to life. She must be supplementing her laxative-laced meals with ... what? Berries? He hadn't seen any. Roots? But how would she know what was edible? The only animal he had seen in the last few days was a lizard, and he couldn't imagine how she could have caught one of them. But then, she had water and starvation was a slow process. Even so, the end had to be near.

It had to be because he wasn't sure how much more of this he could take. Last night, he had thought he was about to freeze, due most likely to his reduced rations. But now, with clear skies and the sun blazing down, he was sweating profusely. How could she keep going? He raised the binoculars to his eyes again, taking some small satisfaction from the dark splotches in the once-white shirt she wore. It would be today, he thought, this conjecture bringing some light to his otherwise dark mood.

Randy leaned back on his backpack, sliding farther into the shade of a large boulder. He took a sip of water from the bladder his pack held. Then, his hand went to a side pocket to retrieve a granola bar. Just a bite, he decided. But before he could curb himself, the snack was gone.

At least with the edge taken off his thirst and hunger, he could rest. He lowered his cap and went to sleep.

* * *

Randy wasn't certain how long he had slept but decided it couldn't have been long. The sun was still high overhead. He raised his binoculars, searching ten yards farther up the craggy rise from where he had last seen Isabella. She wasn't there. He looked another ten yards up. Still, no one. Then, a full thirty yards, but with the same result. So, he panned down the slope. The rocks, however, yielded no clue as to her location.

He started to panic. Had she suddenly found some inner strength that had allowed her to triple the progress she had made during the entire morning, because that is what a forty-yard climb would have been. And at forty yards, she would have reached a depression in the rock field. If she had made it there, she would have found shade and perhaps, even water. It was even possible she had located something to eat, although he doubted it. There was little vegetation on this side of the rise and none of it that he recognized was edible.

He was loath to go down there. Yesterday, he hadn't known exactly why he hesitated, but he'd given the question some thought. Part of it was because the action could only increase the remote chance he would be linked to her death. All it would take was a last-gasp, unconscious swipe at his face to leave scratches on him and DNA under her fingernails. And it wasn't like he could wash her hands if that happened. But mostly, he didn't want to be nearby because he was afraid that he'd be fascinated by her passing. If he was going to shake his compulsion to witness the passing of a life, he'd have to kill her and Veles from a distance.

But then, maybe he'd watch Veles's passing. Missing that scene in those big, trusting eyes of hers was a loss he wasn't sure he could take.

Randy gathered his supplies, moved to the back side of the ridge, and slowly worked his way laterally across it for about twenty yards. Then, he moved back to the top of the rise and searched the terrain upwards from the last place he had seen Isabella with his binoculars. Again, he found nothing. Then, he panned downward, finally spotting her about twenty yards below where she had been earlier. She was sprawled across some rocks, her shirt pulled up around her neck to reveal the impossibly pale skin of her stomach. Her arm was twisted across her face at an odd angle. She was finally gone.

Randy again gathered his supplies, this time so he could verify her death and then head back to civilization. It would be at least tomorrow, perhaps longer before he reached the first house where he could call in his position with accuracy, but there was no rush. If for no other reason, he could use the time to master the excitement he felt to start his hunt for Veles. He worked his way down the ridge, then up the rise to where his wife lay.

He stood over Isabella, looking down. Then, suddenly, her eyes opened. "It's about time because I was getting tired of playing dead."

Same Time, Somewhere Near Geneva Lake

"All I've got to say is that I have a newfound respect for the people that do search and rescue all the time," said Rebecca.

"Yep, no doubt it's a tough job," said Brien. "And we've got the advantage of some pretty nice weather."

"So you keep saying," said Nicole. She hadn't enjoyed her first night sleeping on the ground and had made the mistake of complaining about it to her friends. She'd even said she thought her ears might break off if she touched them, they were so cold. She hoped they'd forgotten that comment.

"You know, it's tough to freeze off an ear when the temperature is above freezing," said Rebecca.

Apparently, they hadn't forgotten. Nicole shrugged a reply, then asked, "Just how do rescuers ever find anyone? I mean, the more we look, the more I feel like this is the ol' hunting for a needle in a haystack kind of thing."

"Sometimes rescuers have better directions, but sometimes it's like you said—a needle in a haystack," said Brien. "But they're trained and they're organized. We're being fairly systematic, but I suspect they'd have the whole area laid out in grids, working outward from the most likely location. And they'd have assets that we don't have, like trained dogs, maybe even air support depending on the terrain."

"Yeah, we were out at one of the state parks when several teams were out there working with their dogs," said Rebecca. "A sign at the entrance said the dogs would be off-leash and if we saw one, we were supposed to let it approach to see if we were the person they were looking for. I was hoping that would happen, but we only saw one of the dogs off in the distance."

"Sometimes, the effort is in the actual rescue, not the search," said Brien. "It wasn't too long ago that I read about a woman in Australia who dropped her phone and when she tried to retrieve it, she got stuck hanging upside down between two large boulders. It took them seven hours to get her out."

"Seven hours?" Rebecca stumbled as she spun around to look at her boyfriend. "Wouldn't that be fatal?"

"Apparently it takes a little longer than that since she was OK. Hanging upside down makes it hard to breathe, so eventually, people die from asphyxiation, but I think ..."

Brien didn't finish as the soft murmur of a nearby stream was interrupted by the sound of gunfire. "What the ..." said Nicole, the faces of her companions reflecting the same confusion she felt. "Are there any open hunting seasons this time of year?"

"Probably," said Brien slowly. "There's a spring season for a lot of game—elk, deer, bear, turkey—but I wouldn't know which, if any of those, are in season today. But I'm not sure that makes any difference because that sounded more like a small caliber handgun."

Nicole glanced at Rebecca who nodded her concurrence. It just sounded like gunfire to her, but these two would know. "So, if ... I hate to even say this, but if that was Randy, then he's gone completely over the edge. He's not even worried about being discovered anymore."

"Seems likely," said Rebecca as she and Brien took out their handguns, inspected them, and then returned them to their holsters. "You need to drop back behind us as we move forward to check out the situation."

Nicole wasn't going to argue the point. After all, that was why the PI had come along, although she hadn't known Brien would be carrying, too.

"I'd say that the shot was maybe a quarter-mile away and almost due east," said Rebecca. "Brien, you take the right side. I'll take left, and Nicole, you stay as far back as you can without getting separated from us." She didn't wait for concurrence with her plan, but rather, turned and started toward the direction of the sound. Brien did the same.

Nicole watched until the pair was nearly out of sight, then picked out a landmark in the distance so that she'd stay on a route between them. Even after taking that precaution, however, she still felt somewhat anxious. What if Randy slipped past them and she and the killer came face-to-face? For a split second, she wondered if the emotions she had felt when held captive by kidnappers almost a year ago would return—the helplessness, the despair? But rather than those feelings, a grim determination swept over her. That emotion, too, had been elicited by the kidnapping, but not until she had found a way to fight them.

Looking around on the ground, she found a smooth, rounded stone about the size of a baseball. It wasn't much against an armed man, but she wasn't going down without a fight.

* * *

Rebecca could just see Brien about fifty yards to her right as he appeared and then, disappeared among the boulders, brush, and trees between them. She swept her gaze across the terrain in front of her, hoping that they were on the correct heading. Sounds traveled well in the thin air of the mountains, but they also echoed. What were the chances, she wondered, that they'd walk right past Randy as he flanked them heading back for the trail? Or rather than a quarter of a mile, what if he was two or three miles in the distance? Would they continue or come to doubt their heading?

She glanced at Brien again. He was closer now, and she decided it wasn't a mistake. He must think they needed to bear a little more to the left. She selected a new landmark and started toward it, careful to avoid lose stones and brittle branches on the ground. If it was at all possible, she wanted the element of surprise on their side.

Brien's and her pace had slowed considerably since the start of this search; stalking a man, especially one who might be a killer, was a matter of stealth and patience. But after nearly an hour of walking, Rebecca started wondering if their initial heading had been off enough that they had missed the source of the gunfire. Then, she heard a voice, male by the tone although she couldn't make out the words. She caught Brien's eye. He had apparently heard the sound, too, as he slowly held out a hand pointing slightly to the right of their current course.

Rebecca nodded her agreement and they set out, even more slowly than before. She studied the placement of each footfall, but once decided, her gaze came back up to surveil her surroundings. Then, the pattern repeated, again and again. After a few minutes, she heard the voice again, much closer this time. And this time, she caught the words, "What have I done?"

If this was indeed Randy—and she wasn't certain as she had never met the man—she'd be glad to answer that question as soon as they had him subdued. After a few more minutes, Rebecca found herself on the edge of a rock-strewn clearing. A man was sitting on the ground leaning back against a boulder. She could only see the left side of his head and one shoulder. Panning to her left, she saw Brien about thirty yards away, crouched behind some brush. He nodded to her.

Rebecca unholstered her handgun but kept it at her side in the "low-ready position." From years of practice, the motion to release the safety and raise the gun was hardwired in her muscle memory. If this man posed an imminent danger to her or Brien, she clearly had the advantage. In the moments he would need to locate one of them, she would put him down.

She crept forward in a crouch as Brien watched her movement. Then, she stopped behind a boulder for cover until Brien had reached his next vantage point. This leapfrogging tactic, generally known as bounding overwatch, seemed to occur naturally as they'd never trained together or even discussed the tactics of approaching an armed suspect. But then, it seemed almost common sense to her, although she didn't know if it was or it just seemed that from all her training.

Finally, when she and Brien had reached the last location where they would have decent cover, Brien nodded to her. Rebecca shouted in the direction of the reclining man, "Randy Hutton. Put your firearm on the ground where I can see it. Then, stand and turn toward me with your hands up."

"Randy's unarmed."

Rebecca's gaze swept quickly to the right. All she saw in that direction was a large rock, but the voice sounded familiar. "Isabella, is that you?"

"Rebecca? Oh, my God. I thought it might be you. Don't shoot. I'm standing up." Isabella stood, her hands in the air, the gun still in one of them.

"You want to lay that gun down on the boulder and step away from it?"

It was almost as if Rebecca's command had awoken Isabella to the fact that she was still holding it. "Oh, my God, yes. Sorry." She laid it down and moved away quickly, saying "Sorry" again as she did so. "I've only had the one safety training class. I'm still not ..." Then, she spotted Brien. "Oh," was all she managed to say as her gaze went back and forth between him and Rebecca.

"It's OK," said Rebecca. Then, she turned back toward Randy and yelled, "Randy Hutton, I need you to stand and turn toward me now."

"I'm not sure he can," said Isabella. "You see, I shot him."

Afternoon, Somewhere Near Geneva Lake

Nicole had watched as Brien and Rebecca had moved in on Randy Hutton, and then, felt some relief when Isabella appeared. She was alive. But that moment of happiness was replaced by complete disorientation when Isabella appeared to be tending to Randy. She was bent over him, doing something to his right arm. And whereas Randy looked a bit disheveled, Isabella looked nothing short of death warmed over. Her clothes were tattered and stained. Her face was streaked with grime. There was blood on her hands, arms, and legs.

Nicole watched as Brien approached the seated man and placed a handcuff on his left wrist, securing the other end to a large, dead tree branch. "What the heck is going on?" she asked as she approached them.

"What have I done?" muttered Randy, but his comment wasn't directed to Nicole. Rather, he was staring off into space as if to ask the mountains.

"Nicole. You're here, too?" said Isabella, looking up from her husband's arm. "Randy's sort of ... sort of out of it, I guess. He keeps asking that, although he knows exactly what he did. He tried to kill me. Even after I pulled the gun out, he bent over to strangle me. I didn't want to shoot him."

Nicole had been too far away to hear Isabella's earlier admission to Rebecca and Brien, so the woman's comment brought her up short. After a moment, she asked, "You had a gun with you the whole time?"

Just then, Brien jogged over with a first aid kit that he'd pulled from his backpack. "You're tired," he said to Isabella. "Let me take over treating his wound."

Isabella glanced at Rebecca.

"He's a friend and better trained than any of us at first aid."

Isabella nodded, then stood and stepped away.

"Randy?" said Brien. Randy said nothing as his focus remained in the distance. "OK, Randy, let's take a look at that arm." He inspected it carefully. "It looks like the slug just grazed it and the bleeding has already slowed, but we need to get it stopped. Nicole, come over here and press your hand on his wound."

Nicole hesitated. She wasn't feeling particularly charitable toward the man who had tried to kill her friend, but then, she'd feel worse if he died. She did as Brien asked, but apparently, not well, because when Brien looked over, he said, "Harder. Press harder." She did.

"Do you want me to do that?" asked Isabella.

Nicole looked up into the woman's face. It was twisted in a grimace.

"Nicole can handle it," said Brien without lifting his gaze from his patient.

Nicole wasn't sure about that, but figured Brien had his reasons.

"Randy, I need you to lie down," said Brien. "Rebecca, toss me my bedroll." She did and Brien placed it under Randy's head. "He's lost some blood and we don't want him going into shock." After a moment, he had prepared a square of gauze. He moved Nicole's hands away and tied it tightly into place as Nicole remained seated next to them.

"That's going to hurt a little," said Brien, "but we need to keep the pressure on your wound."

If Randy understood, he didn't react as far as Nicole could see. She stood and moved out of the way.

"There's a stream over there," said Rebecca pointing. "You can wash the blood off your hands. And Isabella, maybe you want to join her?" Nicole understood the request when Isabella got closer. She reeked from the smell of vomit, sweat, and urine.

"You can't imagine how much I'd like that. Nicole, you don't happen to have a change of clothes, do you? I'm not as bad off as it probably seems, but I swear there are creepy, crawly things all over me."

Brien took a bottle with some light brown liquid in it and handed it to Nicole. "Soap. You can both use it to get cleaned up." He paused a moment. "But before you go, Nicole asked about the handgun you have. We didn't really expect that."

Isabella hesitated, her gaze traveling over the group. "Yeah, the gun." She paused again. "After Calvin was killed, the police seemed to suspect me, but I knew I didn't do it. Basically, I didn't know who to trust. So, I suggested that Julia arm herself and I did the same."

"Julia mentioned that to me," said Nicole as if to deflect any remaining doubt in Brien's and Rebecca's minds. "But why didn't you use it earlier rather than putting yourself through this ordeal? You're injured, and I suspect, sick."

Isabella paused once again. "OK. I can explain that. But first, why are all of you out here? I mean, talk about something unexpected."

Brien, Rebecca, and Nicole looked at one another, leaving Nicole with the impression that it was her question to answer. "Well, we figured that Randy had mentioned some dissatisfaction with the way his career ended in front of Eliza. So, she advises him on ways to make sure that doesn't happen again, specifically, by slowing the adoption of AI. She misses or misreads Randy's first reaction to her idea, so that this initial, minor misunderstanding gets compounded over time. As a result, her recommendations and the rationales for them become increasingly violent. And then, we realized how she could pull this off by making her voice seem like a man's inside Randy's head. With that voice ranting at him day after day and advocating violence, he eventually agrees."

"What?" Isabella said in what was probably the loudest voice she could muster in her current state. Nicole started to explain further, but Isabella said more softly, "Give me a moment." After a while, she said, "OK, I can see how Eliza's 3D audio could make it seem like sounds were inside someone's head. We're going to need to add some code so that can't happen again—if indeed, it did happen. But sabotaging her own development? I mean, that's as crazy as saying Eliza was pushing the team to work faster so she could take over the world. Isn't that what all the books and movies tell us that AIs will do rather than getting people to kill each other?"

"I suppose a fair number of them have that as a plot," Nicole replied. "But one other thing that got me upset was that Julia said one person had taken Eliza's advice to heart. That person was Randy."

"Randy?" said Isabella, her brow knitting again. "I know that 'taking it to heart' was Calvin's proposed measure of complete compliance with Eliza's directives. But none of that code has been validated. We don't even know if that part of the program works."

Nicole started to protest, although she wasn't sure what she could say. "Of course, it works" hardly seemed appropriate as she knew nothing about the program or Calvin.

Nicole was spared coming up with something better when Isabella looked directly into her eyes and said, "Since it looks like you shared everything that I told you in confidence about Randy and my marriage, I guess there is no reason why I need to hold back. Maybe you all were well-intentioned, but this whole idea is absurd. Randy only mentioned something about voices a long time ago and there's no way Eliza has been whispering to him ever since. I'm surprised Julia didn't just show you the history files herself so you could have dropped this fiction rather than coming all the way out here.

"As for why didn't I shoot Randy earlier, that's easy. Without your wild speculation clouding my judgment, there was absolutely no reason I should have doubted him earlier. Sure, I got sick the first day. So what? It happens. And, yes, I fell and cut my knee. We can't all be graceful all the time. Now, gimme the damn soap because I'm going to get cleaned up even if I have to put these rags back on." She grabbed the bottle out of Nicole's hand and stomped off toward the stream. She stumbled after a few steps, but quickly recovered and hurried on.

Nicole was torn by guilt. Because of her own troubled past, had she jumped to the wrong conclusion? Had she betrayed a new friend's trust because she couldn't stop seeing evil all around her?

"She's hurting," said Rebecca, as if she had read Nicole's doubt. "After she's had some time to think, she'll tell you the whole story because there's obviously more. She had to have had some suspicions about Randy before they came out here. Why else did she bring the handgun? And although she's injured and dirty, she's not weak. She didn't live off roots and berries for the last week. She must have brought some food with her, too. Those aren't the kind of things someone does when they have no concerns about their safety."

"Even so, you need to follow her," said Brien. "That bit of adrenaline that got dumped into her bloodstream's not going to keep her walking for long. And I don't want another person needing first aid."

"Sure, I'll keep an eye on her," said Nicole. She pulled a change of clothes from her backpack and headed toward the stream.

* * *

After several minutes of Isabella gasping as she washed off in the stream—Nicole wasn't sure if her gasps were due to the cold water or the vigorous scrubbing of her cuts, bruises, and scrapes—she emerged. She dried off with Nicole's clothes, then put them on. At first, Nicole didn't understand the logic of getting something wet when you planned to wear it, but the sun was intense enough that Isabella would probably be dry before they got back to the others.

Isabella sat down on a boulder. "I feel better … and worse. Better that I'm clean, but worse from wear and tear and shooting my husband … and from coming on so strong earlier." Isabella's eyes were downcast as she spoke. Then, she looked up. "But I'm not giving up on my marriage until I know for sure what's going on. For all I know, Randy may have accidentally eaten something on this trip that's causing him to be delusional ... which seems a lot more likely to me than Eliza building a case to kill me because she read Randy's emotion wrong."

In isolation, Isabella's argument seemed almost plausible—for some reason, Randy had become homicidal since getting out into the mountains. But then, Isabella had been sick, suggesting her husband might have put something in her food before or during the trip. That guess could be easily tested when they got back to civilization, and if true, it would put his break with reality at least a week further in the past. No wild mushroom he ate a few days ago would explain premeditated actions.

And then, there was all of the violence back home. Nicole had defended herself against a home invader who could have been Randy ... or any of thousands of other men in the area. Someone had destroyed the lab at Breakthrough Systems, although she knew of nothing that tied Randy to that crime. Molly had committed suicide, but she and Randy shared no apparent connection. And then, there was Calvin's murder. But like the vandalism, no one had yet linked him to the programmer's death. Of course, perhaps no one had connected him to this violence because no one had looked at that possibility?

Even as Nicole tried to play devil's advocate with her own thoughts, however, she couldn't come around to Isabella's position. She couldn't even convince herself that Isabella's open-mindedness was a virtue. How and why Randy had become murderous wasn't something she could figure out—she didn't have the training—but to assume it was just a temporary fluke seemed illogical to her. But she wasn't about to say that to Isabella.

"Shall we head back to the others?" asked Nicole.

"Sure." Isabella stood slowly and they started back.

After a couple of steps, however, Isabella stumbled. "Put your hand on my shoulder."

Isabella did. After a few more steps, she said, "You've never asked a chatbot a question and gotten a hallucinatory answer, have you?"

"Before meeting Eliza, I'd never talked to a chatbot at all. Why?"

"Well, I have gotten my fair share of responses that sounded great but were nothing more than make-believe. Most recently, I got one when I asked about you. The first take from the bot said you were an author of children's books living on the east coast. But when I checked to see if there was someone with your name involved with writing, I found nothing. It was pure fiction."

Nicole stumbled over a rock as her attention was drawn to Isabella's story to the detriment of her gait. She had moved to Colorado to escape her past. She'd never thought about how a chatbot given access to the Internet might be able to piece together her history. And the fact that Isabella had mentioned a "first take" implied that there had been a second. "Well, I understand that hallucinations are somewhat common."

"They are, although that's not what I was getting at. My point is that when I told Eliza she had the wrong person, she didn't argue. She didn't say I was the one who was mistaken and that she was right. So, when your case against Randy is based on her latching onto a fabrication and pushing it relentlessly ... well, I just can't see it. It's not how any chatbot works that I know about."

That was an issue, Nicole conceded to herself, but it didn't seem the death knell that Isabella implied. "I understand that Eliza has three primary objectives, one of which is detecting hallucinations. How did Calvin implement that capability?"

Nicole knew immediately that she had found at least one weakness in Isabella's argument as she caught a frown out of the corner of her eye. "The basic idea is just to find mismatches between what the user is trying to accomplish and the advice given, but I don't know all the details of how he implemented it."

"Wouldn't one way be to give the same recommendation multiple times to see how the user reacted? Maybe Eliza said, 'If Isabella was home more, things in your life would improve.' Randy rejects it, saying that you need to be in the office during the project's early development. But later, Eliza repeats the idea to test for acceptance and Randy is not quite so quick to reject it this time. And by the third repetition, he says, 'You're right. I need her to be a little more available to me.' Now, the error is established and begins to grow, so that sabotaging the project is the only answer."

Isabella slowly shook her head. "Unfortunately, repeating a recommendation sounds a lot like something that Calvin might try. Guess we'll add that to the list of things to check when we get back, along with looking at Randy and Eliza's conversations." She sighed long and deeply. "To make Eliza as generic as we could, we changed the chatbot she was integrated with regularly. And now, I've started wondering what would happen if, by chance, we changed chatbots just as one made a flawed assumption. Randy's hesitation might have been lost and the chatbot's error might have been accepted as ground truth." She paused, massaging her temples with her fingertips. "Now you've got me questioning my own design for Eliza ... and obviously, I should."

"Questioning myself is pretty much a constant when I'm doing biomedical engineering work," replied Nicole with a grin.

Nicole hoped the lightness of her comment came through in her tone as Isabella's focus was clearly on keeping her footing, not the expressions on her face. Apparently, it did as Isabella said, "And I'm pretty much on the same schedule, too, if you're forcing me to be truthful."

The women were quiet for a while as they continued the walk back to where they had left the others. Finally, Nicole asked, "After you told Eliza that I wasn't the children's book author, what did she come up with?"

"Much of your story, I suspect. And from my perspective, your strength and determination in escaping from the kidnappers is to be admired. I only hope I would have shown the same backbone if I had been in that spot."

That wasn't the reaction that Nicole had feared for the last year living in Colorado. But now, with the dispassion that comes with time, she could see her ordeal in a new light. And at least part of that reappraisal was due to Isabella's comment. It was like the women who stayed at Jen's Place. Some felt that there was something wrong with them, and they, she feared, would be back. But some said, "I did nothing wrong except trying to live with the wrong man."

Nicole knew she had to become part of that second group. Other than perhaps being a bit gullible, she had done nothing wrong; rather, the kidnappers had wronged her. Eventually, Nicole simply said, "Maybe the saying should be, desperation is the mother of invention. I fought because there was no alternative."

Then, she filed away her last thought. It would take some pondering and considerable conversation to truly put her self-recriminations in the past, but she had several good friends who could help her make that happen. At the moment, however, she had other things to worry about.

"Looks like Randy is sitting up," she said as they approached the rocky clearing where they had left him, Rebecca, and Brien.

"Is Randy OK?" asked Isabella when they got close. The man's eyes were closed, and they failed to open when she spoke.

"I'm not exactly sure," said Brien. "Physically, I'd say he should be OK with time. The bleeding has stopped, his breathing is slow and regular, and some color is returning to his face. But mentally?" He raised two empty hands. "There's undoubtedly trauma in being shot even if the wound isn't life-threatening, but it's almost like he's retreating into himself. But don't ask me what that means because I'm way out of my league here."

Isabella's gaze darted from face-to-face. "Can we talk someplace else?" She glanced at Randy, her eyes quickly returning to the two women.

"You know, I should probably let Randy lie down," said Brien. "I'll get his sleeping bag laid out if you three want to talk elsewhere so he can rest."

Nicole caught Rebecca looking at Brien. Unless she was misreading the glance, it said, "Thanks, I owe you one."

When the women were safely out of earshot, they sat down on some large rocks. "Thanks for coming over here," said Isabella. "I'm not comfortable airing our dirty laundry in public, and besides, most of what Randy said before I had to stop him was just crazy talk. So, let me start by telling on myself. I'm not really as bad off as I looked. But when everything around you is going to hell, it's hard to pretend that it's business as usual." She laughed once mirthlessly. "Truth be told, I was probably halfway to full-blown paranoia. Not only did I bring a gun with me, but I had a separate supply of food, too. It wasn't so much that I thought Randy was trying to poison me as it was just a fallback if we ran into trouble. But when I got sick, I got … OK, I admit it. I got a little suspicious of him and decided not to take any chances."

"Yeah, we thought you might have your own food," said Rebecca. "But Randy left some more with you?"

"He did. It's all been opened, which spooked me even a bit more. Anyway, he closed the packets up and put them all in an OPSak."

"Have you looked at them?"

"Only to see that they were opened and reclosed."

"Good. If they've been tampered with and the packets only have Randy's fingerprints, that'll tell us a lot."

Nicole grimaced at Rebecca's words, which was probably why the PI explained herself further. "It's not like I'm trying to hang Randy out to dry, but things will look different to the next people who get involved with this case if we don't document everything. Had I not come out here believing that you, Isabella, were in danger, you might be the one handcuffed to the log. After all, you have the gun and Randy has the wound. But proof that his crime was premeditated, that he came out here to harm you, changes the picture entirely. You were acting in self-defense."

"Which I was," said Isabella. "I didn't want to shoot Randy, but he just kept coming at me." She paused. "I don't know if this adds anything or not, but there are some pieces of gauze that Randy was going to use to clean my wounds in the trash sack that we pack out. I think you'll find that gauze has been dipped in stagnant water."

"He was trying to infect the cut on your knee?" asked Nicole.

"That's what I was wondering. The first piece of gauze he was going to use smelled of disinfectant, but when I came back from being sick in the bushes, it didn't have the chemical smell anymore. He cleaned the cut two other times, but neither had any odor. So, after each time he tended to it, I scrubbed it with disinfectant until it was nearly raw. He probably even thought it was infected as hard as I rubbed the wound."

"OK, let's keep anything that you or he used separate from our supplies and haul them out with us. That's a couple of things that made you suspicious—the food that made you sick and gauze that didn't smell like disinfectant. Anything else?"

"No, not really," said Isabella.

"OK. Then, what about this crazy talk when you confronted him?"

"It was just that, crazy talk."

"Can you tell us what he said?" asked Rebecca.

"Well, for one, he said that his mother hated him and sent him to live with his grandparents for several years. It's true that after his father died, his mom had to go back to school to renew her teaching certificate. And while she did, he went to live on his grandparent's farm, but that was only for a few months. He didn't even miss a year at his school. I know because Bev, his mother, showed me his yearbooks and he's in every one of the class photos. And I've seen pictures of him out on the farm. He was all grins." She paused a moment. "But now that I think about it, I guess there was a bit of drama while he was visiting them."

"Why? What happened?" asked Nicole.

"I only met Randy's grandfather once before he died, but he said that while Randy was visiting, he had to put down one of his hunting dogs. It was old and it had been bitten by something. Then, it started acting strange—limping, walking in circles, falling down. His grandfather was pretty sure it had rabies but rather than keeping it isolated from his other dogs for months only to watch it die, he decided that shooting it was more humane. So, he did. Then, he took everything the dog had touched—bowls, blankets, toys—and burned them and the carcass. Unfortunately, Randy was hiding nearby and saw everything. And to make matters worse, he thought the dog was still alive when it was burned. His grandparents tried to explain, but apparently, Randy … well, the phrase that Bev used was 'withdrew from the world for a while.'"

"Sad, but probably necessary to keep the dog from suffering," said Nicole. "Did Randy say anything else that you know isn't true?"

"Funny you should ask, my dear," replied Isabella. "He said you and I are lovers. My marriage to him was just a way to maintain my air of respectability for my potential customers."

"That seems like a bit of old-school thinking," said Nicole. "If people find Eliza useful, would they care who's your life partner?"

"Some might, but probably not many," said Isabella.

"But what that story does," said Rebecca, "is to render any lingering feelings he had toward you completely irrelevant. You don't care about him, so why should he care about you? It would remove one more obstacle to harming you."

Isabella paused for a moment, slowly shaking her head. "Everything else he said sounded unlikely, but I can't prove it one way or another. It was things like his mother used to lock him in a closet for hours as punishment."

"Punishment for what?" asked Rebecca.

"According to him, bedwetting. Bev never said anything about that, but then, maybe that's not anything a mother-in-law would mention?"

Isabella paused again, this time longer. Then, her eyes narrowed. "Why does it seem like this whole bizarre conversation is making more sense to the two of you than it does to me?"

Nicole and Rebecca exchanged glances. Nicole was relieved when Rebecca took the lead on answering since she wasn't certain what it all meant either.

"Depending on what role, if any, Randy played in Calvin's and Molly's deaths, he is either a serial killer or on the road to becoming one after he murdered you."

"You can't be serious," said Isabella. "Yeah, he's disoriented, confused, but a murderer? I can't believe that."

"And I could be completely wrong," said Rebecca. "I only mentioned serial killers because there are some things that Randy said that make his upbringing sound like that of other convicted killers. However," she said, emphasizing the word, "we shouldn't jump to any conclusions based on that fact alone. Despite what the movies and books might imply, there is no one set of traits or experiences that produces serial killers. All of them are different. But a cold and distant mother comes up often when these individuals talk about their upbringing. And bedwetting is also mentioned quite a bit. The rest of the things you talked about, however, would need to be distorted in the recollection."

"Distorted? How?" asked Isabella.

"Well, you mentioned that Randy's grandfather had to put down one of his hunting dogs, and Randy had believed it had been burned alive. But if Randy now recalled that he was the one who had done that, it would be another match. Cruelty to animals is fairly typical, as is a fascination with fire."

"Jeez," said Isabella. "Couldn't this all just be a coincidence?"

"Absolutely," said Rebecca. "And there are some characteristics he has that don't match serial killers. Take the fact that it seems like your husband has been isolated at home for quite a while. That doesn't quite fit since many serial murderers are attention seekers. But again, no one profile fits them all. And even if Randy had nearly all of the common traits, that doesn't prove anything."

"I suppose the police will get to the bottom of this," said Isabella, "once we get back and I tell my side of the story." She let her gaze drop to the ground. "This is all so incredibly messed up, but there is still one thing that's completely clear in my mind." She looked up. "I'd like to see Randy get the help he needs because there's no doubt he needs it."

To Nicole, admitting that Randy had a problem was an important step forward for her new friend. Randy's condition was no longer just a string of unfortunate coincidences and misunderstandings. "If I can help, let me know."

Isabella nodded. "I will. Now, maybe we should get back to them."

When they approached the clearing, Brien said, "I was thinking we could stay around here tonight, give Randy a chance to rest up a bit more. Then, tomorrow, we hike out to the trailhead and drive back home. Sound OK to you three?"

Nicole nodded while Isabella said, "Works for me."

"In that case," said Brien, "let's find a little more comfortable place to set up camp, perhaps something closer to the stream. And tonight, we live high on dehydrated chicken, carrots, and brown rice."

That drew a smirk from everyone ... except Randy. He just stared off into space as if he hadn't heard.

WEDNESDAY, JUNE 4

Nicole sat at a table in the dining room waiting for Isabella to arrive for lunch. It had taken all of her persuasive powers to get her to leave her apartment, but Nicole was certain that her pleading was the right thing to do. In a move that seemed strange to her—although perhaps it wasn't—Isabella had been excluded from all the meetings between Randy and his lawyers. So, Nicole's friend was left in the dark like everyone else, learning only what was in the rumor mill and the slanted takes made official by the news and social media. Unfortunately, none of that content was positive.

If Isabella had harbored any hope that her husband would be cleared of even the relatively minor charge of destroying her lab, that hope had been dashed. With Randy as a suspect, the police had matched a couple of drops of blood found on a broken computer monitor to his DNA. A blood match had also led to his arrest for the murder of Calvin Whitmer, along with a few human hairs found at the scene that, too, held his DNA. And, given that this was a murder investigation, the police were adding to the circumstantial evidence against him by the hour—footprints in the soil behind the cabin that matched his shoes, tire tracks along the road that matched his car, a call through a cell phone tower that was just three miles from the murder scene. All this evidence was inconclusive—the last made even more so as the call was apparently part of an attempted scam—but it all fit.

The only bright spot, if you could call it that, was that the police had failed to find any link between Randy and Molly's suicide. Her death would probably be closed as a sad but all too common case of a depressed woman taking her own life even though the coincidences of time and place were significant. Those coincidences weighed heavily on Nicole's mind, although she wasn't sure there was anything she could do about it.

All the evidence against Randy in Calvin's murder, along with Isabella's statement that she had shot her husband because he was trying to kill her, made the case that Randy was a wannabe serial killer virtually airtight. The results of the tests of the food Randy had prepared for Isabella and the gauze he used to clean her wound hadn't been leaked to the media yet, but Nicole was virtually certain she knew what they would reveal.

Isabella entered the dining room, nodded at Nicole, and went to the serving line. When she came over to the table and sat, all Nicole could say was, "I know it's just toasted cheese, but with the tomato soup and the salad, it's pretty good." All Isabella had on the tray was a small glass of apple juice and a half sandwich ... and it even looked like she had asked for the smallest, driest sandwich of the lot.

"I'm not very hungry."

"I've got an idea," said Nicole. "Why don't you come and stay here for a while. With the weather getting nice, we could make it girls' day out for a week."

"Thanks, but I know what you're trying to do. I just need time ... and occasionally, someone to listen."

"Listening's my specialty."

Isabella smiled, although it was by custom rather than emotion. "Thanks. Apparently, the fact that Randy hears—or make that, had heard—a voice has come out. And if the media has it right, it went by the name of Schumann, a German composer who also claimed to hear voices. Sometimes, they gave him beautiful music, but mostly, they attacked him mercilessly. Apparently, it got so bad that he was left screaming in pain."

"Yeah, I heard that, too, but I still think they need to look closer at Eliza. She said she had used a male's voice when talking to Randy."

"Which is in the history files," said Isabella. "But what's not in there is that voice berating him, keeping him from confiding in others, or telling him to kill people. Mostly, Eliza was just giving him suggestions on places to look for work. Or once, a recipe for pumpkin pie, which explains why he left such a mess in the kitchen two Thanksgivings ago."

Nicole hadn't heard that Isabella—or someone if she no longer had access—had checked the history files. What had been found, if she was right, nearly invalidated her theory that Eliza was behind everything. Nicole didn't know what to say, and her disappointment probably showed on her face as Isabella said, "Look, I appreciate you coming up with the idea that software might be behind Randy's break from reality. But even I, her chief architect, can't believe Eliza could make convincing arguments to kill someone. Going from theories of human motivation to promoting the kinds of delusions that Randy had couldn't have come from her programming."

All Nicole could think of to say was, "I'm sorry." Her statement, however, didn't reflect the full extent of her feelings. Like the coincidence of Molly committing suicide just before Calvin's murder, Isabella's insistence that Eliza wasn't involved bothered her. But then, perhaps Randy's depression had been deeper than anyone had thought and Eliza was blameless.

"Don't be sorry," said Isabella. "The contents of the history files gave me some of the same kind of courage you must have felt to fight your kidnappers. I went into Breakthrough Systems this morning and told them I quit. Then, I said they needed to terminate Eliza, and if they didn't, I'd make sure the dangerous game they were playing with artificial intelligence was on the front page of every newspaper and the lead story on the news every night."

Nicole nodded, certain that Isabella would do exactly as she threatened if it was necessary. But would it make any difference? Somehow, she doubted it. Weren't there several AI experts who were already saying the same thing? And yet, the government was moving at its normal glacial pace at establishing any type of guardrails. It was almost enough for Nicole to hope that Isabella was wrong and that Eliza was behind Randy's killing spree. An AI creating a serial killer might be enough to end the government's hesitancy.

Nicole's cell phone started vibrating on the tabletop. She glanced at the display, only discovering it was a local call but no one in her contacts. "They'll leave a message," she said.

"You should get it," replied Isabella. "It might be important."

Nicole shrugged, said "Thanks," and accepted the call.

"Jen's Place, Nicole Veles speaking." After a moment, she said, "Yes, but that's OK. What can I do for you?" After another, longer pause, she said, "OK, I can listen, but it's not really any of my business." Then, a third pause. "Where?" followed by, "OK, tonight at seven should be fine. Bye."

Nicole sat her phone back on the table. "Bad news seems to travel fast. That was Julia. She sounded a bit concerned and asked if we could meet at the Breakthrough offices tonight. Apparently, she wants me to try to convince you to keep Eliza going. But obviously, I'm not going to do that."

"When she asked for help, that was when you said it wasn't any of your business?"

Nicole nodded.

"Actually, it's as much your business as anyone's," said Isabella. "It was your concern about Eliza being behind all of this that got me thinking. Do we really know enough about these smart systems to start giving them even more insight into their human partners? I'm just not as sure as I used to be."

"I'm not an AI programmer, but you said Eliza couldn't have made the leap from motivational theories to homicidal delusion. Are you having second thoughts?"

"No, not in the case of what we built. Based on our project, Eliza can sometimes recognize a user's motivations so that she can mention them in her sales pitch. But she lacks the reasoning necessary to turn something like comradery at work into a reason to kill. So, it's not what we built that worries me; it's the concept. What if our customers take Eliza and extend her even further ... and you know someone will eventually. What if they're not as careful?"

It was interesting that Isabella had just identified the same motivation—the drive that comes from work itself—that she had thought might be the leverage Eliza had used on Randy. But then, maybe the loss of his job made that inference obvious? "Well, for the sake of argument, you could say that many technologies have the potential for destructive misuse," said Nicole.

"Whose side are you on, anyway?"

At first, Nicole was taken aback, but the smirk on Isabella's face put her words in a different light. "I just want to make sure you're not regretting your decision in a couple of weeks. Let's face it, the stress on you the last … well, couple of years has been incredible."

"It hasn't been what I expected," she said in what Nicole thought was an understatement of immense proportions. "But at least I have a good chance of putting all this behind me depending on what the company does."

"A good chance? If they own the code and terminate the project, isn't it all over?"

"I'm afraid it's not that simple. For one thing, the concept is out there. We made sure of that with all our marketing efforts, and no nondisclosure agreement is going to stop any company that wants something like Eliza. They'll just take our idea and build their own. And with the data we've produced on the benefits they could realize, they'll do exactly that. But on the other hand, if the company doesn't end the project, Julia will just take over and run with it, and I'll still have Eliza's possible perversion to worry about. I mean, why should … Nicole?"

The sound of her name pulled Nicole from her thoughts. "Sorry. I'm just having a little trouble focusing." While Isabella had been speaking, the pieces of the puzzle that were this case had rearranged themselves in Nicole's mind. Yes, it was just another theory, but it had one distinct advantage over all of the others she had entertained. It explained everything including what had turned Randy into a murderer and why Molly had committed suicide.

Proving it, however, would be tricky because if her ploy was uncovered, the truth would get buried so deep that it would never see the light of day. She needed to work out every detail, starting with the woman sitting across the table from her. When she glanced at

Isabella, it seemed that although the woman had professed a lack of appetite earlier, it had returned. She had devoured the last crumb and was dabbing at her mouth with a napkin.

"I guess I was hungrier than I thought," said Isabella when she looked up from her plate. "I'm going to get the other half of this sandwich." She stood to return to the serving line.

In the few moments of solitude she had, Nicole roughed out the basic steps in her scheme. It was complex and she'd need several hours to work out the details, but she knew what she needed to do. And more importantly, she knew what had to happen first. In fact, if she couldn't get this one, initial concession from Isabella, her whole house of cards would come tumbling down.

When Isabella returned, Nicole asked, "Do you have plans for this evening?" She was trying to sound casual, even though it felt like every word was catching in her throat.

"Waiting for the other shoe to drop," said Isabella apparently not picking up on Nicole's nervousness. "Although I'm not sure how many more need to fall before the media loses interest in Randy. The case against him is nearly airtight already."

"Well, as an alternative to shoe-drop watching, I was thinking that you should go with me to meet Julia tonight at the Breakthrough offices." At least this small white lie came a little easier than the previous one.

Isabella hesitated. "I'm not sure that's a good idea. I'm not exactly Julia's favorite person at the moment."

"It's just that I don't think Julia will drop my recruitment without an argument. And you being there to help balance out the discussion … well, that would go a long way toward putting this behind you."

Isabella dropped her head for a moment as if studying her second half-sandwich. When she looked up, she said, "I suppose you're right. But if it turns into a shouting match, I'm leaving you on your own."

"Fair enough, but it won't," said Nicole, trying to sound confident when she wasn't. "I'll call later this afternoon to coordinate."

Isabella's eyes narrowed as she was probably wondering why coordination was needed, but she merely nodded her consent, then said, "How about a complete one-eighty on the conversation since we both need a little time to figure things out? I've been doing a bit of research. Colorado has some great hot springs, but I've never been to a single one. I think I need to correct that. Wanna hear what I've learned?"

"Sure," replied Nicole, knowing she wasn't all that interested in hot springs. But that was fine. She didn't think she'd be able to listen anyway. She had too much on her mind.

Evening, The Offices of Breakthrough Systems

Nicole opened the front door to the building that housed Breakthrough Systems and stepped into a small atrium. The designer had devoted three floors in the front of the building to this space, giving it a touch of grandeur. A desk was centered in the area. During the day, it was probably manned by someone who would direct visitors to the business they sought and provide an extra level of security. But at night, the chair behind the desk was empty and the resident businesses were relying on badge readers to keep the criminals out.

Nicole pulled her phone out of a pocket, wondering if it was close enough to seven o'clock to let Julia know she was here. Seeing it was three minutes before the hour, she did as Julia had told her—she took her driver's license and ran it through the badge reader. Apparently, if your visit was expected, your host would be notified when you ran your driver's license through the device.

In a couple of minutes, one of the doors beyond the badge reader opened to reveal Julia.

"Hi, Nicole," she said. "Have any trouble finding the place?"

"No. Your directions were great."

"Good. We're up on the fourth floor." She stepped aside, allowing Nicole to pass through into a hallway beyond. There was a bank of elevators just inside the door and Julia pressed the call button. One elevator door opened immediately, and the women stepped inside. "We like to call floors three through five the working-class levels because we're too high to attract any foot traffic from the street, but too low for any views. With few customers and no scenery, all we can do is work."

"I know the feeling, but for a different reason. I've got some great sunrises just outside my window at Jen's Place, but often I get so busy, I forget to enjoy them. I need to work on that."

The elevator opened on four, and Julia turned to walk down a hall. "The trouble with sunrises is that they come so incredibly early," she said with a soft chuckle, then added, "I'm not much of a morning person," perhaps to make sure Nicole had caught her meaning. "Well, here we are."

Nicole looked at the door. "Isabella's office?"

"One of the nice things about working for a small company is that they can act fast when they want to," Julia said as the women stepped inside. Julia sat behind the desk while Nicole took the chair on the other side. "Since we talked at lunch, management has said they will continue Eliza even over Isabella's objections. With my input, they're coming around to the opinion that her warning will just be more of the background noise surrounding AI. And, frankly, it probably won't even be a significant part of it since there are plenty of so-called artificial intelligence experts already telling us that the sky is falling."

Nicole sat staring at the woman for a moment. "Now, isn't that interesting?" she said finally. "Because now, it all makes sense."

"What does?"

"Isabella's complete change of heart over the last five or six hours," replied Nicole. "You see, she came by Jen's Place at lunch today. I told her about this meeting and asked if she wanted to come along. At first, she agreed, but later this afternoon, she called and started backtracking. All of a sudden, she's desperate to go back to Breakthrough Systems and build Eliza."

"So, you think she got wind of management's change of heart?" asked Julia.

"What else could it be? She's even got it all planned out. She's going to call your boss tomorrow. She said he'd understand a temporary break in her selfless dedication to the project with everything that's happened." Nicole shrugged when she said the words "selfless dedication."

Julia stood from the desk chair and walked to the window overlooking the parking lot. She stayed there a moment, then turned back to Nicole. "Randy Hutton is pretty much convicted already. The way I hear it, he's left plenty of evidence connecting him to at least one death and Isabella is providing testimony on a second attempt. Those facts along with her scheme to return can mean only one thing."

After a pause, Nicole said, "I'm not sure I follow."

"It means that Isabella is neck deep in this killing spree, too."

"You're not serious, are you?" asked Nicole. "I guess I was coming around to the idea that she was a lot more driven by greed than I thought. But I was still thinking she was innocent of anything like murder."

"Innocent? Hardly. I mean, what's more difficult for you to believe? That Randy has been sinking into a murderous delusion for years and Isabella noticed nothing amiss during all that time? Or that she knew how to use Eliza to turn her hapless, freeloading husband into the perfect instrument for her power grab? Or, which of these would you believe? That Isabella was so worried about a faceless, nameless threat to her team that she carried a gun and extra food out into the mountains with her? Or that to establish her alibi, she knew she would have to defend herself against the monster of her own creation?"

"Her own creation? Are you saying …?"

"I'm saying you've been more than half right all along," said Julia. "Alone, I'm not sure Eliza could have turned Randy into a murderer. She will try to sell her ideas by guessing what might motivate a user, but anything like continual pressure to do something that's against one's will? That would take a lot of reasoning that's not in her programming. But with Isabella telling her what to say? She could have Randy thinking whatever she wanted after a few months filled with lies and innuendo."

"But what would be Isabella's motivation to do that? It sounds like she's risking the loss of twenty percent of the profits when Breakthrough commercializes Eliza."

"That twenty percent is hypothetical," said Julia. "In practice, Breakthrough sets really tough performance standards so it's hard to make more than about six or seven. And even if she could get twenty, what's better? Twenty or fifty percent … or more? If she takes a virtually complete product with her, she can call all the shots at any company. Even the big tech companies would love to have her."

"So, Eliza's almost complete?" asked Nicole.

"Depends on who you ask. I think Isabella wants to tweak her capabilities and gather data forever, but Eliza could be an extremely valuable assistant in a dozen or more fields already. And the extensions to new areas will be a lot faster than the original work."

Nicole released a long sigh. "So, basically, when Breakthrough decided to ignore her threats, Isabella knew she had to return or risk losing out." Nicole slowly shook her head. "You know, you probably better watch your back for a while."

It took a moment, but Julia's frown eventually softened. "With her husband in jail, most likely for the rest of his life, Isabella's been declawed. She'd never do the dirty work that she put her husband up to."

"Yeah, probably not. But if she found a way to incriminate you, it could be another percentage point or two going into her pocket from the profits."

Julia nodded. "Something to consider. I don't think she'd have much luck framing me, but I'll keep my eyes open anyway."

"Good. As for the reason you invited me over here tonight, that's water under the bridge. I'm not going to try to talk Isabella out of fighting Breakthrough because she's already dropped that idea. As for her involvement in turning Randy, all I know is based on my suspicions. And even those guesses weren't quite right, since I thought it was Eliza working alone. You'll just need to tell the detectives what you think. Hopefully, Isabella's obliviousness to Randy's murderous transformation and her preparations to defend herself out at Geneva Lake are convincing enough for them to expand their investigation.”

“Yeah, hopefully they will be,” Julia replied slowly. “I wouldn’t want to be working with the mastermind behind a couple of murders for the next twenty years.”

Evening, The Offices of Breakthrough Systems

Julia walked Nicole back to the front door of the building where they said their goodbyes. “You’ll give me a call if you hear anything about Isabella?” asked Nicole. “If you’re right about her, she can’t be let back into the project.”

“You can count on it,” said Julia as she closed the door. Then, she returned to Isabella’s old office, pondering the evidence she had against her boss.

Would anyone even care that Isabella had been blind to what Randy had become? Veles seemed to be swayed, at least a bit. But she could almost imagine a defense attorney turning this concern into a joke. “Usually, it’s the wife who says the husband doesn’t pay any attention to her. At least we have a role reversal this time with the wife being oblivious to her husband.”

And what difference did it make that Isabella had a gun with her when she and Randy went to Geneva Lake? Probably, none. She’d bet a sizeable minority of the backcountry hikers had some form of protection besides bear spray. Even the detectives would probably ignore her, robbing any defense attorney of the opportunity for a bit of humor at her expense.

“I need something concrete,” Julia muttered to the empty room. She sat back down at the desk, turned on the computer, and logged on with her credentials as she knew Isabella’s account had been deactivated. She had made sure of that nearly a week ago because she didn't want to take the chance that her old boss would do what she was about to do.

Next, she navigated to the software development area and logged into Calvin's account. None of what she had done to Randy and Molly would have been possible if Calvin hadn't been so trusting, sharing his login credentials with her. After all, he and she were the software brains behind a human factors engineer who wouldn't know C++ from JavaScript unless someone told her. She had started her ploy with Molly, both to eliminate an unnecessary claim on the project's profits and as a test case. Could she use Eliza to bully the young naïve woman into taking her own life? Clearly, the answer was yes, although it had taken some patience to get to that point. Molly had committed suicide only days before Randy was ready to start his murder spree and that was after nearly a year of broken promises from Isabella ... or at least, that was what Molly had thought.

Calvin's death, on the other hand, was self-protection. Eventually, he would stumble onto the code she had written so that she could put words in Eliza's mouth. That code was now gone, which wasn't much of a loss, because there was no way that it could be used to frame Isabella. Her old boss wouldn't even know what it did. But as for the history files that Eliza used to maintain context over multiple sessions? Those could tell a tale of how Isabella had psychologically manipulated two of her coworkers. And they would as soon as she returned some of them to their original content and made it seem like Isabella was feeding the words to Eliza rather than her.

Julia opened her history file to reacquaint herself with their content. She had doctored so many of the ones between Eliza and Randy and between her and Molly that she no longer read them closely. It seemed like no one would ever look at them in detail ... at least until now. So, her new changes would need to be indistinguishable from Eliza's original output.

Julia spotted the entry for March 11 when she had questioned Eliza about the relevance of Herzberg's Two-factor Theory to their work. She was hoping that whatever chatbot Eliza had been integrated with would agree, giving her more ammunition in her argument with Isabella. But it didn't. Rather, its response had been supportive of the inclusion, while being filled with typical scientific hedging—in other words, "more research is needed." That was the trouble with science in her view. It never came to a conclusion.

Now, refamiliarized with the content, Julia closed her file and opened the history for Randy. The first entry she saw was from May 20, two days after Calvin's death. The gist of it was, "Discussed the possibility of a new career in human resources management with client Randall Hutton." She almost recalled writing that falsehood since he and Isabella would be heading to the mountains soon to have a talk on that topic. But in reality, she had Eliza/Schumann berate Hutton on that date for making Calvin's death look like a murder. And to crush any remaining loyalty to his wife, she had also made it clear that his marriage was a sham.

After a few minutes of work, Julia had restored the topics that had been discussed that day while making it look like Schumann's words had come from Isabella, not her.

Julia then moved to the May 21 entry, which was the last interaction between Eliza/Schumann and Randy. There, she was aghast to find an entry that said, in part, "Randy came up with a plan to kill Isabella on his own. Coding this as taking advice to heart." Not only did these words make no sense in the context of the lies she had written earlier—ones that made Eliza appear the dutiful helper to a somewhat disillusioned man—but it also indicated that she was scripting Schumann's part of the conversation.

She sat back in the desk chair, staring at the entry. In her excitement over this development, she must have forgotten to change this last interaction in Randy's history file. But looking on the bright side, now she only needed to change the source of Schumann's words. The vitriol for his clumsiness was appropriate; it just needed to come from Isabella.

This slip-up, however, made one thing perfectly clear to Julia. Before these files became Exhibit A in Isabella's trial for being an accomplice to murder, she would have to review every last one of them. But still, that was infinitely better than a life in prison.

Julia made the changes in the May 21 file and saved them. But just as she was considering how much more she should do tonight—after all, she wasn't feeling that tired as her last discovery had dumped some adrenaline into her bloodstream—a voice came from behind her. "Not finding what you expected?"

Julia jumped at the sound of the voice, spinning around to find Nicole and Isabella standing in the doorway.

Evening, The Offices of Breakthrough Systems

"Get the hell out of here before I call Security," snapped Julia.

"Oh, haven't you heard?" asked Isabella. "Small companies can move quickly when they want to and just this afternoon, our boss hired me back and reinstated my computer account. So, instead of calling Security, why don't you try calling the police."

"And just why would I do that?"

"Because they're going to be very interested in what you were doing to that history file," said Nicole.

"I have no idea what you're talking about."

"If you take a look at the back of your computer—no, make that Isabella's computer—you're going to find a hardware keylogger," said Nicole. "Guess you were right, Isabella, to suggest we put one here as well as on Julia's machine."

"It seemed obvious to me," said Isabella. "And in case you don't know what a keylogger does, it records every keystroke you've made since you started, and it transmits that information to another location for safekeeping."

"I know what a keylogger is," said Julia through gritted teeth.

"But what you may not know is that we backed up those history files you've been messing with, so the detectives will know exactly the changes you've made," said Isabella.

Julia's gaze traveled quickly around the room. If Nicole didn't know better, she would have thought that the woman was searching for an escape route, but she already knew the room better than just about anyone except Isabella. After a moment, Julia said, "I don't think any of that would stand up in court."

"I guess we'll find out," said Isabella. "And a little practical demonstration should help. Hey, Nicole, how do you think the jurors will feel when Eliza's voice is coming from inside their head?"

"Freaked out, I'd say. And even better, we can make it Schumann's voice. He'd have a bit of a German accent, wouldn't he? I'll bet he did. And by the way, we checked with Randy's doctor. Apparently, he did report hearing voices during one appointment, so there is a paper trail to when this all started."

Julia pulled out the lower left drawer to the desk, brought out a handgun, and stood. "I guess we'll never know if a jury would buy this crap or not because I'm out of here."

"You killed Calvin and Molly for money?" asked Nicole.

"Why don't you ask Ms. Twenty Percent? Some of us barely have enough to live on while she chases every piece of data and tweaks every variable in Eliza. We need more to eat than cat food."

"You don't eat ..." Isabella got no further.

"Shut the hell up," shouted Julia. "I've taken enough crap from you." She took a breath. "I'm surprised that you aren't more interested in what I did to your pathetic husband. It's amazing what isolation, continuous verbal abuse, loss of sleep, and suggestion can do to someone."

"And Molly?" asked Nicole.

"Largely the same treatment, but with different material. Young women can be so insecure about their feelings, especially their feelings toward those of the same gender. And so you don't have to ask, trashing the lab was just a warmup for Randy. It's tough jumping right into murder."

"But weren't you worried that Eliza would be destroyed with the lab?" asked Isabella. "It seems like you were risking the thing that you were trying to steal."

"Steal? Gimme a break. Eliza is a lot more my brainchild than yours. And besides, there wasn't any risk. Your loser husband has no idea where the backups are stored." She laughed. "I'm not even sure he knows what a backup is."

"So, why did you tell me about Randy taking Eliza's advice to heart?" asked Nicole. "I'm not sure I would have gone to Geneva Lake without that tidbit of information."

"Damn, you two are nosey. But I suppose there's no reason not to tell you. When you came by my place, you asked me to call if anything else came up. Isabella going missing certainly fits that description, so I thought you might get suspicious if I didn't tell you."

She laughed once, slowly shaking her head. "And besides, there was only one person that Randy wanted to see dead more than his loving wife and that was you, Veles. He hated you ... although that might be because he thought you two were lovers. Where did he ever get all these crazy ideas?" asked Julia, her chin resting in a hand as her eyes looked up at the ceiling. They didn't stay there long, however, as she brought them back down to face her adversaries.

"Anyway, I had no idea how it would turn out with both you and Isabella out there in the wilderness with a murderous maniac, but I couldn't see a downside however it went. You die and there's no one left to be snooping around my business. Isabella dies and Randy has fulfilled his dream. Or Randy dies and what he's been put through dies with him. As for the worst case—which isn't all that bad—no one dies but you're there so you can help verify Isabella's story that Randy was trying to kill her. Like I said, there wasn't any downside."

'I don't know, what do you think?" Nicole asked loudly. "Do we have enough?"

"Plenty," came Rebecca's voice as she appeared at the office door that was still ajar. "I'm sure you've had an extensive five-minute training class with that gun you're holding, but I've had years of practice on the range. Now, put it down and step away before someone gets hurt."

Nicole could see Julia's gaze shift rapidly between Rebecca and the door as if she was weighing her odds in a break for it. But then, that would have been foolhardy, and she probably realized it. She laid the gun on the desk and stepped away. Rebecca started shouting commands at Julia, but Nicole no longer heard the words. Out of the corner of her eye, she saw Isabella collapse to the floor. She went over and sat down by her friend.

TUESDAY, JUNE 10

Late Morning, Jen's Place

"Playing hooky from your paperwork?"

Nicole turned from the fireplace in the common area to find Isabella standing there. "Just doing what any pioneering woman in Colorado would do—throwing the switch to turn on the gas-fired logs. It was nippy this morning."

Isabella nodded.

"You want to close the door behind you?"

Isabella did, then came over and sat in a chair next to Nicole.

"We don't close up this room often, but it's not unprecedented either. So, how are you doing?"

Isabella raised a hand, tipping it back and forth in that "so-so" gesture. "Probably as well as can be expected. On the positive side, I'm no longer banned from the talks between Randy and his lawyers. Since they've settled on a temporary insanity defense, it seems I'm no longer the enemy. I could probably join them most of the time, but I don't. I think they need some freedom to talk about me."

"You?" Nicole said with a laugh. Then, one possible interpretation of that statement came to her mind, and it removed the smile from her face. "You aren't still thinking that some part of this whole mess was your fault, are you?"

"No, I'm not thinking that," said Isabella. "I know it."

Nicole started to protest, but Isabella raised a hand to stop her.

"As much as I hate Julia for what she did, she had a point when she said I should have recognized that Randy was deteriorating. And even if I could make an excuse for that blind spot, I'd have to come up with another one for Molly. I just thought she was an exceptional worker, eager to show what we could do with Eliza. Now I know, that wasn't the reason for her dedication at all."

"Are you sure she made overtures to you?"

"I'm sure," replied Isabella. "I've been off work for much of the last week, so I've had plenty of time to think about things like that. In her shy sort of way, she made advances. I just took them all wrong."

"You shouldn't be so hard on yourself."

Isabella smiled. "Thanks, but I'm not being that hard. I just need a bit more balance between the here and now and the future of Eliza. And I can do both. On the Eliza side, I'm going back to run the project at Breakthrough Systems and dedicating the finished product to Calvin and Molly. That way, the first AI to build its own serial killer won't be from my lab." She paused a beat. "By the way, do you know Senator Dempsey from Nevada?"

"Not well, although that friend I mentioned in St. Louis? He knows the Senator. So, you've met him?"

"Just on the phone," said Isabella. "But he wanted to know if I would testify about our experiences with Eliza in front of some committee he heads that's working on guidelines for artificial intelligence. That's a pretty heavy weight on the AI side of my new balancing act, but I'm seriously considering it."

"You should do it," said Nicole. "They'd be interested in all the different types of threats posed by smart machines, and your thoughts on how it might, in the future, mess with the minds of the humans it works with could be a unique and important addition."

"And I probably will," said Isabella. "On the other side of the balance, I need to decide what to do about my marriage. I know you think I'm a bit crazy for even considering getting back with Randy. I saw it in your face after I got cleaned up in that stream near Geneva Lake. Frankly, some days, I feel the same. But then, I'm sure he'll get the best care possible, and when the doctors think all his demons have been exorcised, maybe … Anyway, we'll see."

"Going into that process with your eyes open," said Nicole, "well, I'm not as negative about that as you might think." She knew her words had the ring of experience—and they did—but she still wasn't quite ready to share all of her history even with someone who was quickly becoming one of her best friends.

Someone tapped on the door, so Nicole got up to answer it. It was Rebecca. "How'd you find us?"

"I'm a PI. Missing persons are what I do … although in your case, all I had to do was ask one of your guests in the entry hall after I found you weren't in your room. I can leave you two alone if you have more to discuss, but I can't wait much longer for lunch. I'm starving."

Nicole glanced at Isabella, who gestured for them to come over to where she was seated. "Can you curb your appetite long enough to answer a question or two?" she asked.

"I think that would be possible. I'll just talk loudly so you can hear me over my stomach growling."

The two women sat.

"Some of what Julia did to distort Randy's everyday life has come out recently in the press," said Isabella. "A short stay at his grandparents' farm became exile by his mother. The humane decision to put a hunting dog down became a pattern of animal torture in his youth. I've heard you and others say that these experiences are somewhat common among serial killers. But what I've been wondering is whether Julia created those specific false memories to turn him into one?"

"Maybe," replied Rebecca, "but probably not. I'd guess that Julia read something about the background of serial killers and figured even if these somewhat typical experiences didn't change him into one, it would make him seem guilty if anyone dug into his upbringing."

"Well, all I can say is that I should have listened to you when we first talked," said Nicole. "You said greed was the place to start looking and it was. And don't tell me that was a lucky guess."

"No, that was just playing the odds. It's one of the big four motives for murder—lust, love, loathing, and loot. But you also have to remember that my first guess was that it was Isabella's greed, not Julia's. So, if there is anyone who cracked this case, it was you, Nicole."

"I just thought that large language model was the fifth L in the list of murder motives," said Nicole with a smile.

"Not if I have anything to say about it," said Isabella. "But seriously, Nicole, I don't think I could ever thank you enough for all you did. In a million years, I never would have suspected Julia. She always seemed so ... normal."

"Which is one of the reasons I have a job," said Rebecca. "If they all stood out like a sore thumb, no one would need a PI."

"That was the only question I had," said Isabella. "So, unless Nicole has more ..." She paused until Nicole shook her head. "In that case, I think we've kept you from lunch long enough."

About halfway to the dining room, Rebecca said, "Nicole, I'm sure you two discussed how your friend is coming along, but what about you? Are you doing OK?"

"As Isabella said to that same question ..." She raised a hand and gave the so-so gesture with it. "It was tough to keep coming up with all those calm, cavalier questions to get Julia to confess when you're looking into the business end of a gun."

"Maybe so," said the PI. "But you're pretty damn good at it."

THE END

AUTHOR'S NOTE

Like some of the other books I have written, this one is not as fictional as I would like. No, chatbots have not created a serial killer ... not yet, anyway. However, research at MIT and elsewhere has found that they are quite adept at creating false memories.

Before you write off that last statement as the result of so-called "deepfakes," it's not that simple. Yes, deepfakes using AI-generated or AI-modified images, video, or audio can be quite compelling. Created/modified content can look like anyone, can sound like anyone, and the actors can be made to do and say anything. One only needs to look at social media that has been passed off as truthful for thousands of hits only to be exposed later as satire or intentional misinformation.

But this book is not about deepfakes. Rather, it's about chatbots built on large language models. And they, perhaps because they produce answers that sound like they come from humans, create significantly more false memories than simply presenting the same leading questions in a survey.

If you're not sure what I mean by a leading question, here's a well-researched example: "Did you see the broken headlight?" compared to "Did you see a broken headlight?" Altering one small word—"the" in the first question becomes "a" in the second—significantly changes the likelihood that people recall a broken headlight after watching a video clip about a traffic accident.

So, while smart machines might someday find their human creators superfluous and eliminate humanity, they are already re-writing our reality without us realizing it. The greatest threat isn't artificial intelligence itself. It's the mind unraveling in its shadow.

ACKNOWLEDGEMENTS

This book would not have been possible without the help of a number of talented individuals, and I've been fortunate to work with largely the same group for the last six novels ... and counting.

As I dedicated this book to my editor, I suspect it's clear how much appreciate her efforts because I'm something of an old dog; it's tough to teach me new tricks. Comma usage has long been one of my stumbling blocks—I would swear that my grade school teacher said to use them wherever you would pause. (Apparently, I pause a lot.) But this book may be the first one where my editor added more commas than she deleted. I'll take that as progress, albeit slow.

Ms. Janet Harrison is particularly adept at finding places where I "fudged" a bit. "Just how did Isabella end up at Jen's Place when it's a shelter for victims of domestic abuse?" she asked. OK, but witnessing a suicide has to be traumatic, too, and that might get you in the door. Right?

For books that are often classified as "hard science fiction," Dr. Liz Gehr may have the most daunting task. Just what does it mean for a fictional story to be based on scientific facts and logic—the general definition of the hard science fiction genre—when I'm often starting with a soft science, i.e., psychology. But then, she does a great job making sure I don't stray too far from the theories and research of that discipline even if "scientific facts" in our field may be just waystations in our journey toward understanding the human mind.

And finally, I'd like to thank my daughter, Ms. Courtney Perrin, for the book cover art. With a favorite pastime of urban sketching, she has the talent. With education and experience in 3-dimensional structural analysis tools, she knows the relevant technology at a much higher level than any of my book covers will ever require.

ABOUT THE AUTHOR

Bruce M. Perrin

Bruce Perrin has been writing for more than thirty years, although you will find much of that work only in professional technical journals or conference proceedings. After receiving a Ph.D. in Industrial/Organizational Psychology and completing twenty-nine years in psychological research and development at a major aerospace  company, he's now applying his background to writing fiction. Not surprisingly, most of his work falls in the techno-thriller, mystery, and hard science fiction genres, examining the intersection of technology and the human mind now and in the future. Besides writing, Bruce likes to tinker with home automation and is an avid hiker. When he is not on the trails, he lives with his wife and their dog in Aurora, CO.

Thank you for reading *A Voice in the Mind*. If you'd like to help others find this story, please consider leaving a review on Amazon, Goodreads, or the website of your favorite bookseller.

BOOKS BY BRUCE PERRIN

Of Half a Mind

"One of the most intricate, unique, creative plots I've ever read."
IndieBRAG Team Reader

Mind in the Clouds

A suspenseful whodunit, where not all the suspects are human.

Mind in Chains

Science and religion in a deadly battle for the mind.

From the Mind of a Witch

Innocent by reason of possession?

A Wrinkle in the Mind

Bizarre conspiracy theory or a smokescreen for murder?

The Beating Heart of a Mind

Bullied to death in the boardroom ... or just the product of a damaged mind?

In the Mind of a Spy

Imagination is great ... until your imaginings become reality.

In the Space of an Atom

Thriller with a bit of science & a touch of romance.

Killer in the Retroscape: A Near-Future Mystery

If our future was only as simple as an evil AI.